ALWAYS BEEN YOU

NOAH & EMMA

THE KERRIGAN FAMILY
BOOK 3

ANDREA FINNELLY

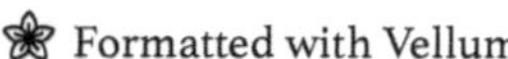 Formatted with Vellum

CONTENTS

1

"Why can't I have a life where I can sleep in?" Noah Kerrigan groaned from underneath the blanket. His alarm buzzed for the second time, prompting him to hit the button to make it stop.

He wasn't a man who stayed up all night partying. But any night he spent with his twin brother Luke and their friend Sean watching some sporting event together, he ended up dragging himself home too late. The morning came too early for him to be comfortable.

He didn't understand how his twin did it. Luke slept three hours every night and he was still able to function like a normal person. Noah figured it had something to do with his time in the military.

As for Sean, Noah was always teasing him to get a nine-to-five job somewhere just so he could suffer along with the rest of them. His friend was an artist and set his own hours. So he slept in and often didn't wake until hours after the sun had already risen.

The bastard.

Thinking about Sean shifted his thoughts to his friend's

sister, Emma. She was always on his mind lately. Okay...if he was being honest, she'd been on Noah's mind since about the time she hit twenty-two. He was three years older than Emma and had always thought of her as a pesky little girl who would hang out with them, tagging along or causing trouble with his cousin, Ryleigh.

Then that one night changed everything.

"Hey, Sean, isn't that your sister dirty dancing with the guy we met on the beach?" Tim Larson, their buddy from high school, asked.

"What? What is she doing here with that loser? I'm going to lock her in her room. She's too young and naïve to be here dancing like that, and he's no good for her."

Noah watched Sean stalk over to Emma, who was dancing with some guy who, in his opinion, was dancing a little too close to her. Not that he cared any more than he did for his female cousins. Though he never thought Marinda, Katia, or Ryleigh couldn't take care of themselves. If he even hinted they couldn't, they'd have set him straight real quick.

As they observed Sean, they realized things were about to get out of hand.

"That's not going well. Think we should go make sure Sean doesn't kill the guy?" Noah asked.

Tim glanced over at him. "Might not be a bad idea."

They both rose from their seats and walked over to the trio.

"...loser. Stay away from my sister," Sean was saying to the guy. They were standing straight up to each other, neither one backing down.

"Maybe your sister doesn't want me to stay away, if you know what I mean."

"I'm going to fucking kill you if you touch her. Got me?"

Noah and Tim each grab the men to stop them from getting into it right on the dance floor.

"Come on, Sean, Emma can take care of herself," Tim said.

"That's what I've been telling him, but he won't listen. Take him home and sit on him, will ya?" Emma asked.

Tim dragged Sean away, still spouting off that they were going to talk about this later.

Noah stuck around for a little while longer to make sure Emma was okay.

"I'm fine, Noah. You can go too," she said to him.

"Actually, I think I'm going to go. No offense, babe, but I like my women without any complications," the guy said before taking off to the other side of the club where a group of women were hanging out.

Emma stood still for a moment with her mouth open. "What an asshole!" she said, crossing her arms.

Noah agreed. How could a guy treat someone as sweet as Emma Cooper that way? "Need a ride home?"

"Yeah...that'd be nice. Thanks, Noah."

They walked out of the club and to his car together. Opening her door, he waited until she got in before closing it. Once he settled himself in the driver's seat, Noah started his car then turned to Emma.

"You're still staying at your parents' house?" he asked.

"Yes. I'm supposed to move in with Sean in another month, but I'm not sure I want to now that he's acting like I need a keeper," she said disgruntled.

"He just wanted to help, Emma, but even I think he went overboard," he added.

The rest of the drive was done in silence. When he pulled into her parents' driveway, he put it in park and turned to her. "You going to be all right? With Sean, I mean." He wasn't going to let her deal with his friend on her own if she didn't want to.

"I can deal with Sean. I'll just sic my mother on him. She'll set him straight about how I'm an adult and he doesn't need to look out for me all the time anymore," she said.

"Okay. Have a good night."

"Thank you for helping tonight and for driving me home, Noah."

Emma reached out a hand and placed it on his arm before leaning forward and giving him a chaste kiss on his lips. As if realizing what she'd done, she quickly unbuckled her seatbelt and opened her door.

"See ya," she said as she left the car, closed the door, and ran to the house. Noah sat in shock before shaking himself out of it and heading home.

Noah jumped out of bed after remembering that time five years ago. He wasn't the only thing getting up. This shit needed to stop. He had been thinking of all kinds of scenarios about him and Emma ever since.

It wasn't a place he could go. Not with her brother being one of his best friends. He wouldn't like how Noah thought of his sister and the things he'd like to do to and with her.

Stepping into his bathroom, he turned the shower on, making the temperature bitterly cold, removed his boxers and stepped inside. Standing in the cold water until he got himself under control, Noah turned the knob to warm it up, taking the small amount of time he had to wash himself. Turning off the water, he stepped out, grabbing the towel off the rack and drying himself off.

Standing in front of the mirror, he finger-combed his dark brown hair. He kept it short, though not as short as his brother did. They were mostly identical...mirror images of each other. And yet, no one who really looked would mistake one for the other.

Noah had a slim, lean look. He was muscular, but not like Luke. Luke was in the military for longer than anyone liked. Even after being home for a while, he was bulked up with muscles. He also had a harder look about him.

Noah wished things were different, yet the things Luke most likely experienced during his time in the Army made him someone who rarely laughed anymore. Now Luke was the sheriff, while Noah was a doctor at the local clinic. It was good to have his brother back in Cypress Bay with him.

After brushing his teeth, shaving, and throwing on some aftershave, Noah walked out of his bathroom, a towel wrapped around his waist, and stopped in front of his clothes rack.

His bedroom didn't have a closet. Instead, he had a clothes rack with one side of shelves standing against one wall. It was his own fault. When Ryleigh asked why he didn't want one, Noah told her he didn't have many clothes anyway, so what was the point? Now he wished she had put one in.

Maybe he should give her a call and let her add a closet, but he was too busy to care.

His parents owned the building, and he talked them into letting him rehab and rent the upper floor after he came home from medical school. The apartment was a loft above their office and one of the downtown stores they rented out. He liked that it was near the clinic, and was happy with the short walk to work.

Of course, he didn't rehab the apartment himself. He could intricately sew up any wound or navigate in the smallest area of the body during a surgery procedure. Hammering a nail into wood...not his thing. He totally talked his cousin, Ryleigh, into taking over the rehab and paid her to make it habitable for him. Best decision ever.

The loft apartment boasted his master bedroom suite on one side, a guest room, bathroom, and small office on the other side, and the center was one big open space that included his kitchen, dining room, and living room.

Ryleigh left the industrial pipes in the ceiling and softened it up with wood panels behind them. It made the black piping stand out against the lighter color of the wood ceiling. The floors were made of the same wood.

They opted to keep the brick walls and instead made the kitchen white to balance out all the darker tones. The street views were amazing. He had floor to ceiling windows that allowed him to view the entire downtown district and, on a clear day, all the way to the lake.

Ryleigh had wanted to add a second-floor loft with additional rooms and a catwalk looking down into the living/kitchen area, but Noah nixed it. He liked the tall ceilings. It made it seem more open, like there was more space that allowed him to breathe without feeling closed in. It was his sanctuary after a long day at the clinic or at the hospital in Pine Grove when he was on rounds.

Snapping himself out of his thoughts, Noah grabbed his keys, locked the door and sprinted down the stairs to the street-level landing he shared with the store on the first floor. They had a door that would take him out to the street and one that led out the back to their parking lot.

With such a nice day, he decided to walk to the clinic, pushing through the front door and coming out onto the street.

He thought about the clinic. While he didn't own it, he worked with the owner, an older doctor, who he liked and respected. Dr. Sid Mancera had been a staple of the town for all of his life, opening the clinic well before Noah was born. As Dr. Mancera told it, he had stopped by Cypress Bay with his wife as they were on their way to Orlando for a conference. They really liked the quiet area, the proximity to Orlando, and soon realized there wasn't a place for people to go for quick medical issues.

At the time, residents had no choice but to go to Pine Grove for the local doctor or hospital. So he and his wife came back a few months after the conference and opened up the clinic, where they did everything from giving wellness exams and vaccines, stitching up a nasty cut, to setting a simple broken bone. More complex issues still had to be transported to the hospital, but they were now able to stabilize the patient first before the ride.

At the clinic, they performed X-rays, EKGs, respiratory

testing, and more. They accepted walk-ins for any minor emergency or to make an appointment for primary care. Other than his regular patients, Noah enjoyed that he never knew what he would be taking on each day.

Stepping into the clinic, he greeted the intake specialist, "Good morning, Allison."

"Good morning, Noah. You have your first appointment in room 2. Leann is your nurse today. No walk-ins yet," Allison Grant informed him. He didn't know what they would do without her. She was a dynamo at keeping the schedule and making sure patients moved through the office as fast as possible.

"Well, it's still early," he replied as he walked past her and down the hall to his office. Putting on what his mother called his "doctor coat", Noah walked out to the hallway, washed his hands, then plucked the patient file from the door before knocking and entering.

"Good morning. What can I do for you?"

2

Later that morning, Emma Cooper slowly woke up, blinking at the sun streaming through her windows. Damn, she forgot to block them again. She meant to close the blinds. But by the time she came home, she was too tired to think about it.

Getting out of bed, she walked to the bathroom to prepare for the day, her mind already thinking about her projects and what needed to be done once she got to her shop. She had several projects at different stages that would need to be completed.

Typically, she produced glazed pots, vases, and bowls, which she then sold in a local store in downtown Cypress Bay. They tended to sell well with tourists and locals alike. But she also liked to experiment with other things for fun, like ceramic jewelry and tiles. She would often receive commissioned work, too.

Lately though, she was feeling restless and thought she would like to let out her more creative side with sculptures and wall art pieces.

Throwing on a tank top, clay-stained jeans, and topping it with a light flannel shirt, Emma left her room to the main living area. Her brother, Sean, would still be asleep. He was an artist and preferred to work in the sunroom, which didn't get the right light—according to him—until the late morning and early afternoon.

She lived in the house she had bought with Sean. They were both self-employed, and it took some finagling to be able to purchase the small home. She wasn't sure if they would have been able to manage it if it hadn't been for the fact it was a fixer-upper, or if Noah and Luke's parents hadn't helped them. They owned a lot of commercial properties in Cypress Bay, but also acquired homes that needed work. When they heard Emma and Sean were looking for a place to buy, Mr. and Mrs. Kerrigan went with them, bought the house they wanted, then set up a payment plan they could afford.

She would forever feel as though she were in their debt. They wouldn't want to hear it, but that was how she felt.

Together, she and her brother pooled their funds and had Ryleigh come in and renovate the house, while they added in their own time to help out.

It started as a three-bedroom, two-bathroom home with a large room in the center that had nothing—no kitchen, no flooring, no lighting. It really was a disaster.

Once they were done, the home boasted two master suites, each with their own bathroom and walk-in closets, a half bath for guests, a gorgeous main room with a kitchen, living room and dining room, and the sunroom that Sean used for his painting.

Walking into the kitchen, Emma opened the fridge and pulled out a bottle of orange juice and a yogurt. What she wanted was a large breakfast of eggs, bacon, and toast. It wasn't that she couldn't eat it. She wasn't on a diet or anything. She just didn't like to cook, preferring it when Sean was up and cooking for them both. Not that he cooked all that much either.

Her ideal someday would be to find a guy who got up in the morning and had breakfast ready for her.

Emma sighed at the thought. At the rate she was going, that was never going to happen. She went out with her friends in Orlando on occasion to the clubs, but honestly, the guys she met were not the kind to wake up and make her breakfast in the morning. The rest of the time she was holed up in her workshop.

Which reminded her that she needed to leave the house and drive to work. Taking her juice and yogurt, she placed them in the bag she kept on the hook by the door, before pulling it down, grabbing her keys along with it. She left the house, locking up behind her, and walked to her car.

Her car was another relic.

She bought the small Mini Cooper as a lark, seeing as her last name was Cooper. She thought it was funny. Her brother thought it was ridiculous, which made her love it even more. But the car was also old. She couldn't afford a new one, so she bought the used car when she was seventeen, having saved up all her money from her pottery sales from the time she was fifteen. The car was about on its last legs now, but she didn't care. It was her baby.

Starting it up, Emma thought about her work on the drive out to her workshop.

Unlike the troubles they had buying the house, Emma was able to afford to rent out a small warehouse to work with her pottery. She needed a place that would allow for her kilns and the space for multiple shelving units to accommodate the various stages of her pottery. The warehouse was a bit out of town, but she liked to keep to herself, and this took her away from disruptions while she was working.

The kilns, tools, and supplies she often used were expensive, too. Especially for someone just starting out. Lucky for her, she was able to find a used kiln at first. After a while, she was able to upgrade it. She kept the original kiln as a backup and for additional firings. Her parents also gifted her some supplies and tools over the years for her birthdays and Christmas gifts. Now, she had a fully stocked workshop ready for whatever project she was working on.

Today, she would be finishing the final touches on the small gift she made for Oliver and Demi to give them at their engagement party. She'd need to think of something special for their wedding present and start on it soon, too.

She had made something for Simon and Aylin for their engagement party—everyone knew it was an engagement party except for Aylin, who didn't find out until Simon proposed that night. They married without telling anyone, so Emma wasn't able to plan a gift, but Oliver and Demi would have an actual wedding...or so they said. Emma wasn't going to miss creating something special for their big day.

By the time Emma pulled into her workshop parking lot, she knew exactly what she would be working on. Getting out of the car, she grabbed her bag and walked into the workshop, ready to start the day.

Stepping into her workshop always gave her a thrill. Most people would turn up their noses, but Emma loved the smells that hit her first thing as she opened the door. Despite the added ventilation, the building still had a damp, earthy smell to it, along with a hint of sulfur and other burned metallic fumes from using the kiln. After a while, the scents faded into the background as she worked.

If asked to describe the scent to others who had never been in her workshop, she would need to say it was like being in the middle of a swamp and the forest. If an industrial building were placed in the center of it.

Okay, so maybe it wasn't a pleasant smell, but she loved it all the same.

Still, she had to be safe. Especially when using the kilns

because they gave off carbon monoxide, and she often used materials that were toxic. Since her shop didn't have any windows, it was essential to have huge fans in the ceiling and around the back wall where the kilns were located to suck out any dangerous fumes. She also had carbon monoxide detectors just to be on the safe side.

Emma rarely stuck around the back area while the kilns were running, preferring to work at the front of the shop until her pieces were done firing.

But this morning wasn't for firing work. That she'd save for later in the day. Now she'd finish up the piece she started for Oliver and Demi's engagement party, before turning to the creation of a new piece for their wedding present. Walking through her workshop, Emma started gathering everything she would need to start her work.

3

Little did Noah know that he would eat his words about it still being early for walk-ins by that afternoon.

He was exhausted.

It had been a long day of running from one patient to another. He normally loved it, but later in the morning they had an unruly patient who went ballistic when Noah tried to examine him.

The man had come in complaining about abdominal pain, but something else was going on, too. The man was obviously having some sort of hallucinations, which made him believe they were all after him. The man started throwing things all over the room, and Dr. Mancera had to come in with a sedative, while the rest of them tried to wrestle the man under their control enough for him to administer it.

Unfortunately, his nurse, Leann, was injured by some of the flying objects. Noah patched her up and sent her home, asking Allison to call in Marcy, who was off for the day. They had three nurses—Leann, Marcy, and Violet—who all rotated days between him and Sid. He didn't like having to call anyone in on their day off, but it couldn't be helped. Violet couldn't handle both his caseload and Sid's, so Noah had no choice but to call in their third nurse.

Now she was acting like a child, pouting, sending veiled insults and guilt trips about how it was too bad she didn't get to finish whatever it was she was doing at home.

Noah really didn't give a damn.

She signed on at the clinic knowing she might be called in at any moment. The last thing he needed after the day he had was having to deal with her attitude.

Marcy was new to the area. Unlike Leann Simmons and Violet Taybor, she didn't grow up in the Cypress Bay area. Most of the people who grew up in the quad-town county of Cypress Bay, Pine Grove, Riverview, and Tola Beach were laid back and kind of just went with the flow.

Marcy was as out of place as the tourists who descended on the lake town each year. She wore too much makeup—he'd never figure out how the hell it didn't all melt off in this heat—and when she wasn't in scrubs, her clothes left little to the imagination, and her nails were like claws, which he thought would make it difficult for a nurse to do her job properly. But she never seemed to have a problem.

He admitted she was a good nurse despite the attitude she was throwing around today.

"Can you check with Allison and see if there's anyone waiting to be brought back?" he asked Marcy, while he finished up some notes on the patient he just left before moving on to the next one.

"I guess. I'd rather be hanging out at the lake, but I suppose I can see if there are any more old people in the waiting room," she said petulantly.

"Marcy. You can either do your job without snide comments or we're going to have a problem. Got me?" Noah snapped, his teeth clenched so tight he thought they would crack.

"Sure," she said offhandedly before walking through the door to the reception area.

What the hell was he going to do with her? He'd need to talk to Sid later about her attitude. He couldn't continue working with a nurse—no matter how good she was—if she acted like a child when she didn't get her way. And if a patient ever heard what she just said, that would be bad for the clinic.

One thing Marcy was right about, there were a lot of the older population of Cypress Bay regularly coming into the clinic. Noah didn't have a problem with it. Most didn't have serious medical problems. They were mostly lonely.

And for those who did have an issue, he was glad they were able to help them in time. With the hospital a town away, someone having a heart attack had a greater chance of dying before they arrived. Now with the clinic in Cypress Bay, they were able to stabilize a patient before transport arrived to take them to the hospital. The survival rate increased exponentially after Dr. Mancera opened the clinic.

After the unruly patient this morning, he'd take a day full of the older patients every day.

Finishing up the paperwork on the last patient, Noah knocked and entered the next room. "Hi, Mr. Lassiter," he said, welcoming the older gentleman, who used to be one of his middle school teachers.

"Noah! Nice to see you, young man. Boy, you've grown since I last saw you."

Considering he last saw him when he was twelve, that was saying something, Noah thought. "Yes, sir. What brings you in today?"

He listened to the older man, taking care of him by examining the issue and referring him to a specialist in Pine Grove for further tests. Once finished, he left the room to find out what was up with his nurse and any new clients.

Noah shook his head when he thought about Marcy. How

she managed to keep her job when she acted like a petulant child was beyond him. Apparently, she didn't act like one around the other doctor. And since he was the owner of the clinic and the one who hired the staff, it made sense that she wouldn't act that way around him.

But she was getting on his last nerve with her attitude.

After going into a couple of more rooms to visit with other patients, Noah went searching for Marcy. She should have been in the rooms with him to make the appointments go more smoothly, to help him with taking notes, and to get him supplies when he needed them. Instead, she was nowhere to be found.

Turning the corner, he spotted the supply room door open and strode over to it with purpose. Stepping inside, he saw Marcy with her hands full of supplies.

"What are you doing?" he asked.

"Oh, you startled me, Dr. Kerrigan," she said, almost dropping the supplies.

"If you haven't noticed, we have patients that need assistance," he said, his eyes narrowing at her.

"Of course, but some of the rooms were getting low on supplies and I decided to refill them while you were busy with the old people in rooms two and three," she told him.

"Your job is to be in the rooms with me to assist when needed. Go drop off those supplies, then get back to the patients," he ordered. "I'm sure there are people in the waiting room who need to be brought to a room to be seen."

"Yes, Dr. Kerrigan."

"I'll be in my office. Let me know when the next patient is ready," he ordered.

Satisfied Marcy would get back to work, Noah turned and walked to his office to write up the notes for the patients he had just seen.

4

The workshop was exactly how Emma had always wanted it. It took a bit of time to earn the money needed to fix it up, but it finally had the exact flow she needed to work in.

She had stations set up around the perimeter of the workshop for each stage of her process. The center of the workshop held an island with a sink, mini fridge, coffee station, utility bench, and a desk for administrative tasks.

When needed, clay and other supplies were delivered on semi-large pallets. For this reason, she had a garage door located on the right side of the workshop next to the main door. It led into a small storage area, where the clay and other items sat until she prepared it for use.

Emma glanced around her workshop in satisfaction. She had a station to work on things like tiles and where she would create some sculptural pieces. There was a shelving unit just past that for those projects to dry.

Beyond that were her turning wheel and another shelving unit for those items to dry before being prepared for the kiln. Just past the kiln, at the back of her workshop, was a staging area. Every item she made was set on a shelf after coming out of the kiln until she was ready to prep it for glaze, decoration, and finishing on the left side of the workshop. In front of those areas was a shelving unit that separated each stage.

Emma had an area for final touch-ups, photography—with a mini photography studio setup with a table, backdrop, lighting, and camera to document every piece she created—and packaging, where she had another garage door. She could pull up a truck, usually borrowed, to load up her wares to bring into town when they were ready to be sold.

Lastly, in the far corner was a little half bath with a toilet and pedestal sink. It was the only "room" in the workshop that had its own walls and a door, but completely necessary when she spent all day working. She was glad she ate the expense of having it put in; otherwise, she wouldn't be able to spend as much time in the shop working. And that just wouldn't do.

At the moment, she was in the process of taking the bowl she made for Oliver and Demi off the drying shelf and preparing it to be bisque-fired in the kiln. This was the first time it would go into the kiln until she glazed it. Satisfied with her prep work, Emma opened the heated kiln and slowly placed it onto the internal shelf.

Most of the time, she would fire it up for more than one item, but this was the only project she had ready at this stage. Once it went into the oven, she'd move her attention to decorating some of her other pieces. She wasn't a painter like her brother, though she could hold her own when it came to decorating her pottery.

"Shit!"

Emma quickly pulled her arm out of the kiln after pushing the gift she had made for Oliver and Demi into it. She couldn't believe that she had done it again. She looked at her arm as the red mark appeared along with a few blisters. With a sigh, she closed the kiln door, then walked over to the island sink, turned on the faucet and stuck her arm under it.

This wasn't the first time she had burned herself, and it wouldn't be the last. After leaving her forearm under the cool water for fifteen minutes, she turned off the water, then gently dabbed her arm with a clean towel from the cabinet under the sink. Grabbing the first-aid kit with her other hand, Emma opened it up and swore.

"Great! That's just what I need," she said to herself, forgetting she'd used the last of the burn supplies in the kit about a month ago.

Emma had been meaning to replace them, but obviously she forgot. That meant she needed to go to the clinic and have Noah look at it. Maybe if she was lucky, Dr. Mancera would look at it instead and Noah wouldn't need to know.

If Noah found out about another burn, he would yell at her to be careful, and then he'd call Sean and tell him to yell at her, too. After this, she just might have the entire Kerrigan clan yelling at her. Especially since the engagement party was this weekend and all the Kerrigans would be present.

She didn't like leaving her kiln running while she was gone, but it couldn't be helped right now. She'd drive over to the clinic, have her burn taken care of, then come right back. Locking up her workshop, Emma walked over to her car and gingerly got in. Her arm was beginning to hurt now. Maybe she should have kept it under the cool water longer. Figuring it was too late now, she started the car and drove herself to the clinic.

Once there, she went in and walked up to the reception desk. "Hey, Allison."

"Emma. What happened?" Allison asked.

"Umm...I sort of burned myself," she said, not wanting to admit it.

Allison gave her an exasperated look. "You know Noah won't be happy to hear you burned yourself again. And after today, I'm not sure he has the patience to be polite about it."

"What do you mean? What's going on?"

"He had an incident with a patient this morning, and Leann got hurt," she explained. "He's not in a good mood."

"Well, we don't need to bother him. I don't mind seeing Dr. Mancera," she said. This just might be her lucky day.

"Nope. I'm not going to be the one getting yelled at because I sent you to Dr. Mancera instead of Dr. Kerrigan. He'd have my head, so you'll just wait for Noah and take your lumps now instead of later," she scolded Emma.

Guess she wasn't so lucky. She blamed growing up around the Kerrigans. With so many of them—and being one of the founding families of Cypress Bay—anyone close to them was considered part of the family and therefore was treated as if they were by everyone else in town.

Allison was a local, having lived here for most of her life, and that meant there was no way she'd let Emma see anyone but Noah. The town watched out for those who were part of the Cypress Bay original families.

Crap!

"Here, fill out this paperwork and sit until you're called," Allison ordered.

Emma grumpily took the clipboard and pen, sitting down in the seat across from her. Fine, she pouted to herself. She'd handle seeing Noah and take his censure. No problem.

After a few minutes, a nurse she had never seen before called her name, directing Emma to a room. "Hi, are you new here, Marcy?" she asked, reading her name tag.

"I've been here for a while," the nurse answered vaguely as she took her vitals.

"Oh, Noah didn't mention the clinic hired a new nurse. Of course, I haven't been in here for a while either," Emma responded.

The nurse seemed to perk up at her mentioning Noah. "I actually moved to Cypress Bay recently and was lucky enough the clinic was in need of another nurse. Dr. Kerrigan hired me personally," the woman said slyly.

Was she insinuating Noah was involved with her? She'd know if he was seeing someone, right? Of course, she would. The entire Kerrigan family would be over the moon if any of them were seeing someone seriously. They threw a huge party for Simon and Aylin, and this weekend they'd throw another for Oliver and Demi. No one in the family got away with everyone in town knowing a Kerrigan was involved with someone.

"It's so nice working with Dr. Kerrigan. He's amazing," Marcy continued.

Emma felt a little weird about how the woman said this, but Marcy didn't say or do anything that made her think she should be feeling that way. She was sure Noah was amazing to work with. That was just what she meant.

She stopped her train of thought at the knock on the door. Noah entered, closing the door behind him. He gave her a heated look before masking it. No, that couldn't be right. She was just imagining things. Noah would never look at her with anything other than like a little sister or cousin. "What did you do to yourself this time, Emma?"

Sighing, she knew what was coming would be inevitable. "I burned myself on the kiln again. I wouldn't even be here, but I ran out of my medical supplies and forgot to refill them."

He shook his head at her. "Well, let's see what you did to yourself."

Noah walked over to her and gently removed the towel she had wrapped around her forearm. "Emma," he scolded when he saw it. She admitted that it looked worse now than it had when she was at her workshop. The area was deep red, shiny, and had a series of blisters running down in a line.

"It doesn't look like it's infected, but I'll put you on an

antibiotic as a precaution. Marcy, get me the burn cream, the non-stick gauze, and a gauze wrap," Noah requested.

"Sure, Dr. Kerrigan," Marcy cooed.

He looked up sharply at her tone and narrowed his eyes at her before directing his attention back to Emma. *Hmmm...now that was interesting. Maybe he's not involved with her after all.*

He spoke with Emma as he cleaned and tended to her burn. "Are you and Sean going to the engagement party this weekend?"

The nurse stiffened her body slightly at how Noah asked, but since Marcy quickly relaxed and continued working, Emma thought she must have imagined it.

"Of course. I'm making a gift for Oliver and Demi, which I was working on when I burned myself," she said wryly. "I'm not sure about Sean. You know how he is, but he'll most likely be showing up with his latest muse."

He smirked and snorted at that. Her brother was a notorious playboy. He never stayed with the same woman for more than a week—even that was pushing it. He called them his muses. Sean was shameless.

Finishing up, Noah gave her burn care instructions. "You're good to go." She rolled her eyes because she'd heard it all before. "I know you know how to take care of a burn, but I still need to go over the instructions. It's procedure."

"Okay, okay. I get it, Mr. Doctor," she teased.

Noah laughed. "I'll see you this weekend, Emma," he said with a look in his eye that Emma didn't understand before he left the room.

She hopped off the table and grabbed her purse to follow the nurse out of the room.

"So, is Sean your boyfriend?" Marcy asked.

Emma laughed. "Oh no! He's my brother and Noah's best friend." Just the thought that someone would think Sean was her boyfriend or that he would even have a girlfriend was humorous to her.

The nurse said, "Oh, that's right. Noah's mentioned Sean before. He sounds like a nice guy."

"He is." Emma might need to reconsider the relationship between Noah and his nurse. Why would he tell her anything about Sean?

"It sounds like your brother is seeing someone then. His muse?" Marcy asked.

"Not really. He just kind of casually dates," she replied.

"Here's Ms. Cooper's chart, Allison. Take care of the burn, Emma," Marcy said, abruptly changing the subject and ushering Emma out into the reception area before closing the door behind her.

Emma left the clinic confused about many things. What was up with the nurse? And what were those looks from Noah? It reminded her a bit of the look she caught him giving her last month when he and his brother Luke were over watching the game at their house.

Knowing she wouldn't figure it out standing on the sidewalk, Emma walked to her car, intending to go back to her workshop. She would probably never understand what all that was about. It didn't matter; it was time to get back to work. Pulling out of the parking space, she drove away, leaving her thoughts about it all behind.

5

That weekend, Noah drove himself to the Cypress Bay Manor Resort for Oliver and Demi's engagement party. The family resort was owned by all of the Kerrigan cousins, having ownership recently turned over from their fathers who owned it before them. Though Simon, Oliver, and Marinda were the only ones who worked there on a daily basis. Ryleigh sometimes came by to help with repairs. The rest of them— Noah, Luke, Katia, and Hailee—had jobs outside of the resort, but came by as needed for meetings.

As he walked in, he noted that the decor was as over the top as it had been for Simon and Aylin's engagement party. Instead of blue and silver though, the colors around the room were a deep green and gold.

Looking out over the expanse of the room, Noah spotted Oliver and Demi surrounded by Simon, Aylin, Joel, and Uncle John, while the new couple was congratulated by those already at the party. Demi was wearing a dress the exact shade of green with gold shoes and accessories to match the decor and her engagement ring.

He didn't know how the girls did it again—and he'd bet

everything he had that Oliver and Demi didn't have a clue until they arrived. His cousins, Marinda, Katia, Ryleigh, and Hailee, did the same thing last year with Simon and Aylin's party, matching her dress and the decor to the ring on her finger, without anyone being aware of it until the actual party. At the time, Noah thought Simon was going to wring the girls' necks since he hadn't even asked Aylin to marry him, nor had she seen the ring. At least this time Demi already had the proposal and ring.

Walking over to the group, Noah grasped each of the men in a one-arm hug, giving the women full hugs. "Congratulations, you two. I see MarKatRy and Hailee found your colors," he said with amusement.

Saying the triplets' names in one sentence was always a mouthful, so the guys came up with the abbreviated MarKatRy for whenever they had to mention them all together. Marinda couldn't stand it, Katia tolerated it, and Ryleigh loved it.

"Yeah. I went shopping with them and didn't even realize until we walked in here they were directing me toward this specific dress the whole time. The little stinkers," Demi said, scrunching up her nose.

"You'd think we would have learned after what they pulled with Simon and Aylin," Oliver added.

"No way you could have known. You had already proposed by the time this party was planned. It's not like you had a secret or anything. They almost ruined everything with our party," Simon said disgruntled.

"Hey, it all worked out. I had no clue until you put the ring on my finger," Aylin reassured him.

Oliver and Demi excused themselves when they saw some people they wanted to talk with. Uncle John—making a production of dragging Aylin laughingly with him—went to sit down with Noah's parents and other aunts and uncles, at what they lovingly called the parent table.

Noah tried to pay attention to the conversation he was having with his cousin Simon and Simon's friend, Joel, but his eyes kept shifting over toward the doors. He was waiting for the moment when Emma Cooper walked in. The anticipation of seeing her again made his heart race.

And then it happened. She walked through the door, and he couldn't help but stare as Emma entered the room.

She wore a short, flirty long-sleeved black dress with lots of long silver necklaces. Her short hair was styled and clipped back on one side with a silver barrette. His cousin, Ryleigh, stepped up next to her. Those two were thick as thieves when they went out. But right now Noah couldn't even tell anyone what his cousin was wearing, or that she was with Emma at all. He felt like his tongue was hanging out of his mouth at the sight of Emma.

She took his breath away.

Emma was like two sides of a coin—one side wore clay-stained clothes, while the other side loved to dress up for a night out of mischief with his cousin.

Noah excused himself for a moment to grab a drink. His mouth was suddenly dry and in need of moisture, as if he were in the desert instead of the conference room at Cypress Bay Manor Resort.

Once he had his drink, he walked to the other side of the room where his view of Emma was better.

Luke sidled up to Noah, resting his back against the wall. "You need to be careful staring at Emma that way. If Sean ever finds out, he'll kill you."

"I don't know what you're talking about," he said, shifting his gaze away from her and out to everyone else at the party.

"Speaking of Sean, is it awkward that he's taking your nurse out on a date to Oliver and Demi's engagement party?" Luke asked, taking a sip of his drink.

Noah looked around until he spied Sean with his nurse,

Marcy. He didn't even realize that his friend was dating her. Or that he planned on bringing her to the party. "Yeah, it's weird. Marcy has been asking me all kinds of questions about Sean ever since Emma came by the clinic the other day."

Luke straightened off the wall. "Let me guess, Emma burned herself again. How bad was it this time?"

"Second degree. She needs to be more careful, but she won't listen to me. She wouldn't have even come into the clinic if she hadn't run out of supplies in her medical kit."

Noah was exasperated. Yes, she had the experience to take care of it herself, but he wanted to take care of her. No, he'd rather she took care of herself by making sure she was safe when using her kiln. Barring that though, he wanted to be the one she went to when she needed help.

Allison told him later that Emma had tried to have Dr. Mancera attend to her burn over him, trying to avoid his lecture on being careful. What she didn't realize was that no one in the clinic would send her to anyone but Noah. She was part of their family, and everyone knew they took care of their own.

What no one knew—except maybe his brother Luke, damn their twin senses—was that he had loved Emma for most of his adult life. Noah wanted her in his life, but he was resigned that it most likely would never happen. Because Sean would kill him.

"Hey, it's my favorite cousins!" Ryleigh exclaimed as she and Emma walked up to them. Luke snorted at that, and even Noah chuckled, despite not realizing they were headed their way. Ryleigh always said that whoever was with her was her favorite.

"Hey, brat. What trouble are you two up to today?" Luke asked affectionately.

"Us? We don't know what you are talking about, Luke. Isn't that right, Emma?" Ryleigh turned to her friend to ask.

"Absolutely no trouble out of us, Sheriff," Emma said, trying to keep a straight face.

Ryleigh and Emma looked at each other and burst into laughter. Noah shook his head at them. They always got into some sort of trouble together. Nothing major or illegal. More like cars breaking down, getting themselves in the middle of others' fights, stuff like that. They'd all had to 'save' them on more than one occasion.

"Emma, you've outdone yourself with the gift you made for Oliver and Demi," Luke said, as Sean and his date sidled up to them.

6

"Hey, sis. I agree with Luke. It's a great piece," Sean complimented her.

"Thanks, guys," she replied, eyeing his date. What was she doing at the party with Sean?

"Oh, you made something? I'd love to see it," Marcy added.

Emma felt a little uncomfortable talking about herself and her work around the nurse. Something was not sitting right with the woman. She was a little uneasy at the clinic talking about the party and Sean, then suddenly her brother was bringing the nurse with him to the party as his date? What was up with that? At her confused glance, Noah shrugged his shoulders at her. Guess he was as surprised as she was.

Her brother wasn't a choirboy or anything. He dated a lot of women, but it still seemed pretty strange to her the way this all happened. Of course, it was most likely just a coincidence. The nurse was new to the area, and with Sean's dating history, it was just a matter of time before he took her out on a date. That had to be it.

"I showed it to you, remember. The bowl with the green and gold swirls," Sean reminded his date.

"Of course, the bowl. It was...nice," the woman said, with a slight tip of her mouth as though she was amused by Emma's work.

"Thanks," she replied dully, more confused than ever.

Emma was already feeling her energy draining just being in a crowded room, even if she considered most of the people at the party to be as close as family.

"How's your burn?" the nurse asked her.

"Burn? You burned yourself again, Emma?" Sean asked, his exasperation coming through.

What the hell! Why would she bring that up here? Or at all, for that matter. "It's nothing. No worse than any of the other times. And it's good. Thanks."

"You're still wearing the bandage," Noah commented as though he had just noticed it under the filmy long sleeves of her dress. "You should have already been able to take it off. Come on, let's go over to the table and I'll take a look at it."

"Do you need my assistance?" Marcy asked.

"Uh...no. This shouldn't take long. Why don't you all continue to enjoy the party, and we'll rejoin you later," he said, eyeing Emma with a knowing look.

She didn't understand what that look was for, but she didn't want to ask about it or start a scene with everyone looking on. "Fine, let's go and get this over with."

Noah brought Emma to a table in the corner, away from other people. "Why did you bring me all the way over here just to check on my burn?"

He looked at her briefly. "It seemed like you were getting uncomfortable, and to be honest, so was I. So I thought it might be nice to use this as an excuse to take a moment away from everyone."

Emma was thankful Noah recognized she wasn't comfortable and needed to take a minute by herself...or in this case with Noah. Something just wasn't right with his nurse, but she couldn't put her finger on it. It seemed Noah was about as confused about the situation as she was.

"I really do want to look at your burn, but I don't have a first aid kit on me. If I remove the bandage here and you need more care, I won't be able to do anything about it. You have two options. We can stay at the party, rejoin everyone else as soon as we're ready, and you can come by the clinic tomorrow so I can check out your burn," he began.

"What's the second option?" she asked.

"We can rejoin everyone when we're ready and, after staying for an appropriate amount of time, we can leave the party so I can check out your burn at my apartment," he said, still holding onto her arm.

The look he gave her could only be described as nothing short of scorching. She didn't imagine the looks he'd been giving her after all. Emma wasn't sure what to think. She couldn't say there was never a time when she'd thought the same about him. She'd admit to having a crush on all the Kerrigan boys at one point or another, but there was always something about Noah that kept her coming back to him.

She wasn't about to mistake what he was asking with the options he gave her. Apparently, he felt as much lust for her as she did for him. She didn't doubt that he'd take a look at her burn. It would be the first thing he'd do, but the second option he gave her held so much more meaning than just checking her burn.

Did she take it? Even knowing nothing would come of it? There was no way she could ever become involved with one of the Kerrigans other than as friends. Her brother would kill any one of them who touched her. But what he didn't know wouldn't hurt.

"Emma?"

She was going to go all in and take the chance. "Option two."

Noah smiled at her, and she knew she had made the right

choice. After discussing what they would do so no one would be suspicious when it was time for them to leave, they rejoined the others, going their separate ways in the crowd.

Despite having a lot of fun, the party seemed to drag on and on. All Emma thought about was leaving the party and going to Noah's apartment. So he could examine her burn. That was all he wanted to do. But she couldn't get the looks he kept giving her out of her mind.

Finally, with a glance and a nod from Noah, Emma left the room to go to the restroom before meeting him outside by his car.

She thought she would be nervous as she slipped out of the room, while Noah walked over to his family to say his own goodbyes. But it was as if everything started to make sense. The looks Noah had been giving her, the bolt of energy she felt around him. She had the hots for him for sure. If only lust survived over the long term and also helped control an older brother, who had a thing about his friends hitting on his sister.

No matter. This would be a one-time thing. Something to remember. They'd share looks with each other when they all gathered at the home she shared with Sean to watch a hockey or baseball game.

Satisfied with that outcome, Emma slipped out the back door and walked around the building to Noah's car, where he was already waiting for her.

7

Noah was going to hell!

What was he thinking, telling Emma to come to his apartment? He was definitely playing with fire, and he was the only one who would be getting burned. Probably set by her brother and his friend, Sean. But he couldn't help himself. He'd been in love with Emma for too long. The opportunity presented itself, and he grabbed it before he had any second thoughts.

He drove through the streets of Cypress Bay until he came to the parking space behind his downtown building. As a thought occurred to him, he turned to Emma. "I forgot to ask, how did you get to the party?"

"Ryleigh picked me up. I should text her and let her know I left," she told him.

"Good idea," he said as she pulled out her phone and texted his cousin.

"Okay. That's done," she replied, looking at him. "We should go in before someone sees us sitting here."

"Sure. Of course." What was he thinking? Even though his

entire family was at the engagement party, there were other loft apartments and businesses still open. Anyone could look out and see them. It was dark, but the parking lot for residents and business owners was well lit.

Of course, it wasn't like they were doing anything wrong. Noah was simply checking on a friend's burn.

And that was a lie. The last thing he was thinking about was Emma's burn. But he'd go with it if anyone asked him about her visit.

Getting out of the car, Noah directed Emma into the building, up the stairs and into his apartment. Once inside, he led her over to the kitchen counter. "Why don't you have a seat at the island while I grab the first aid kit?"

At her nod, Noah went down the hall to where he kept his first aid kit and used the time to center himself. He needed to calm down. This wasn't the time to let her know he was unable to control himself.

Grabbing the medical kit, Noah walked back down the hall and froze in the doorway. Emma was sitting on the barstool at the island in only a black camisole slip.

Damn, he was surely going to hell. And there was no way he could control himself now. He only hoped she wouldn't notice. He untucked his shirt to cover himself, walked to the kitchen, and sat on the barstool next to Emma, turning it to angle toward her.

"Let's see the burn," he strangled out. "Um...what happened to your dress?" he asked as he proceeded to unwrap the gauze to check out the burn.

"I tried rolling up the sleeve, but I couldn't get the cuff over my arm. So the only other option was to take off the dress. It's not like this isn't decent," she said, looking down at her slip.

"Yeah. Right. That makes sense," he stuttered out, trying to concentrate on the burn on her arm instead of how the top of the slip wrapped around her breasts, highlighting her cleavage, or how the bottom of it was rising up her thighs.

Concentrate, Noah!

In making himself look at the burn as a professional—yeah, like that was going to happen—he noted that it did look a little better. "Have you been taking the antibiotics and putting on the burn cream?"

"Yes."

"Okay, so why do you still have the gauze bandage around it?"

"Honestly, I forgot to take it off after work. I've been putting a bandage on to protect it while I work, and then I take it off when I get home to let it air out. I just didn't think about it tonight," she explained with a shrug.

"Okay. Let's leave it off now. I'll put a layer of burn cream on it, and you can let it air out some more. It really does look like it's healing well."

"Sounds good," Emma replied.

When Noah was done, he hurried away from her and into the kitchen to the fridge, opening it. Was it hot in here? He just needed some air to cool himself off, he thought. "Do you want something to drink?" he asked, not looking over at her.

"A whole bunch of shots will do," she said.

"What?" Noah twisted his head to look at her. He was taken aback by her reply for a couple of reasons. First, he was surprised by her answer in a dry tone. He knew she drank alcohol, but she'd never had anything but beer when he was around. And she only had that beer every once in a while, never hard liquor.

Second, she wanted to do shots...was that a good idea? What if she got plastered? How would he explain why she was in his apartment overnight to Sean or to anyone else who questioned him? Despite his better judgement, Noah agreed.

"Actually, let's do it," he said, wincing as he realized how those words sounded.

He could use some liquid courage himself. Hopefully, it would help him resist her further. Dull the senses and all that. Setting up some glasses for shots, Noah pulled down a few bottles from his cabinet. "Whiskey, vodka, or tequila?"

"How about we start with tequila and see what we want from there?" she replied with a smirk.

What was she up to? Noah had a feeling she knew something he didn't. It wouldn't be the first time the women in his life had things planned out behind everyone's backs, and it most likely wouldn't be the last. Considering the two engagement parties, he figured the women knew how to keep a secret or two.

"Tequila it is then. No limes though," he said while setting down the other bottles on the counter and pouring them each a glass of the tequila."

"That's all right. Who needs them anyway?" she said with a wink before downing her drink in one gulp.

"Right," Noah replied before downing his own drink. This was going to be a long night, he thought as the liquor burned down his throat. He hoped his ability to speak in complete sentences that made sense would come back before he had to be at work tomorrow.

He refilled the glasses one more time and turned to grab some chips, emptying the bag into a bowl. No reason to do this on an empty stomach.

"Why don't we move to the living room...you know, in case we get too tipsy and fall off the stools," Emma suggested. Picking up both of their glasses, she walked over to the couch and sat down. "Are you coming?"

Noah thought about it for a moment. Did he really want to do this? The tequila from the first shot warmed him from the inside out. Fuck it. He was doing this. Grabbing the bottle of liquor and the bowl of chips, he walked over to her. Setting them down on the coffee table, he stood over her, grabbed his glass from her hand and gulped it down in one mouthful.

He was so going to hell after Sean got ahold of him.

8

This was a bad idea, but Emma couldn't help but feel like this was the only way to knock down Noah's resistance to her.

She was confused about her feelings for Noah when she witnessed him staring at her at the party. Add in how he looked at her at the clinic and in her home when he came to watch the game months ago, well, she thought he was confused about how he felt toward her, too.

He probably thought she was some innocent little girl, but she wasn't. Yes, she was an introvert, but that didn't mean she hadn't dated or slept with anyone. She had slept with men without getting attached before.

Besides, it wasn't like she was in love with Noah. She just wanted to have sex with him, to find out if that helped clear up her confusion. More than likely they would have sex, realize it was good—oh gosh let's hope it was good...it had been a while for her—decide it was a nice one-time event and move on. They'd pretend it never happened and everything would go back to the way it used to be when she was pretending not to notice him looking at her like he wanted to eat her up.

She just needed the liquor to break down Noah's resistance

and give her more courage to get things going. She felt so out of her comfort zone.

Who knew he actually had a cabinet full of liquor? Noah was a bigger surprise than she imagined. Could it be he wasn't as straight-laced as everyone thought? He may be a busy doctor, but he was also a Kerrigan.

Emma swallowed down her second shot as he sat down next to her on the couch. She could do this. Besides, what's the big deal with sleeping with Noah? It wasn't as though her brother didn't sleep with every available woman around. He may have even slept with one of the triplets for all she knew. Okay, Emma knew he never had sex with any of them, but seriously he couldn't blame her for wanting Noah. He was sexy as hell. He was lean and built.

And yes, some may ask why she wanted to sleep with Noah. Why not Luke? They looked exactly alike—well, almost exactly alike. As teens, they could barely tell them apart, but since Luke went into the military, he came back with a shorter haircut and more muscles than a bodybuilder.

Noah's hair was slightly longer, as though he always needed a haircut. He was muscular too, but in a more streamlined way. There was no confusing them with each other anymore.

Besides, she never thought of Luke in the same way she thought about Noah. Her thoughts were all in good fun. She never expected to actually be here with him like this. She'd never even been to his apartment before. And here they were taking shots and talking about her work and the clinic.

After a few more shots, Emma started leaning closer to Noah. She didn't know if it was because she wanted to be closer to him or if she couldn't keep herself sitting up straight any longer. It had been a while since she'd had a bunch of shots. The last time was a couple of years ago with Ryleigh at a club. But they were dancing all night and drinking a glass of water between each shot.

Emma glanced up at Noah. He was giving her that look again...like he wanted to drag her down to the floor and have his way with her. Well, she'd let him at this point. Staring up at him, she lost her balance and began to tip over. She grabbed at Noah as she fell, landing on the floor between the couch and the coffee table, pulling him down with her. He fell on top of her, as unsteady as she was after drinking more than a few shots himself.

"Oof." Good grief, he was heavy, she thought. But she also thought it felt great having him lying on top of her. He was solid to her soft, and he made her feel surrounded and safe. His arms came up, so he rested on his elbows around her head, hanging his head over her and again staring into her eyes. The heat in his stare had her shifting under him restlessly.

Damn...there was that look again. It did funny things to her insides. Like butterflies fluttering around. Or maybe it was from all the alcohol. One or the other. She moved her arms to wrap around his neck, her fingers spearing into his hair, holding on tight.

Before she knew it, Noah was kissing her. No, it wasn't just a kiss. He was devouring her, his tongue dueling with her own, his teeth and mouth nipping and sucking at her lips. It was sloppy and messy. And she loved every moment of it.

Funny how if someone else tried this with her, she'd probably throat punch him. But with Noah, it was like nothing else she'd ever experienced.

"Bedroom. Now," he demanded, slowly getting up and pulling her with him.

They staggered together across the room and down the hallway, throwing off clothing along the way to his bedroom. Not releasing each other, they fell on the bed in a heap, Noah's mouth traversing her body. He sucked her nipples, one after the other, until they were tight and beaded. Emma squirmed at the sensation, clutching her legs together as though it would bring her the release she craved.

He slid down her body. "Open your legs for me," he growled.

She immediately did so, giving him space to move in between. He used his fingers to open her up and instantly latched onto her clit with his mouth.

"Ah, Noah!" she cried out. She clutched her hands in his hair, moving in sync with his tongue and lips until she finally broke with an intensity she had never experienced before.

He slowly and lightly licked around her as she came down before crawling up her body and taking her in another soul-seeking kiss. This one was slower and deeper than their first, as though he were savoring her.

The tip of his cock brushed against her core until he surged inside. Oh god!

Her first thought told her it was like coming home. Her second? No way this was going to be a one-night stand.

9

Early the next morning, Noah was just waking up, his head aching with a slight hangover, when he suddenly had a bad feeling about the night before.

Please tell me I didn't sleep with Emma, he thought.

He knew full well that he did. He only wished he didn't. His next thought was that if she wasn't in bed with him, then he could pretend it never happened and move on with his life. Like that would happen, but he could pretend.

Noah turned over in bed, and Emma was sprawled out next to him, hugging one of his pillows to her chest. Damn it...he was most definitely going to hell. Sean was going to kick his ass and kill him, and then he was going to hell.

But damn it was the best sex of his life. He may have been drunk, but he knew exactly what he was doing. He just kind of hoped that when he woke up, it wouldn't be true so he could live another day. There wasn't any way it could have been better, other than it not being with Emma. Mostly because of the Sean thing, not because he didn't want her. Because he did want her...and now that he'd had sex with Emma, he didn't know how he would be able to get her out of his head.

Not wanting to wake her, Noah slowly rolled out of bed and went into his bathroom to prepare for the day. In the middle of brushing his teeth, a thought occurred to him. With his toothbrush clenched in the side of his mouth, he opened the bathroom cabinet, pulling out his trash can.

No condoms. Damn it! Shit! This was not happening.

Maybe he left it in the bedroom? Gross, but he was drunk. Tiptoeing back to the bedroom, he looked around the bed, the floor, and the night table.

Still no condoms. Crap.

They had sex several times throughout the night, and he didn't use a condom once. He was a doctor and knew better. Not that he didn't trust Emma. He did. But it wasn't just diseases they needed to be worried about. They also needed to worry about her becoming pregnant.

With that thought, he walked back into the bathroom, opened the shower door, and turned the water on before turning back to the sink to finish brushing his teeth. When he was done, he jumped into the shower. He'd just play it by ear and see how Emma wanted to deal with this. And by this he meant sleeping together. Maybe it would be all right and they'd keep it to themselves. No problem.

The rest of it they would need to talk about when she got up. No point in worrying until there was a reason to worry. Noah finished up in the bathroom, got dressed, and went out into the kitchen.

In the meantime, he would make some breakfast for them. Emma liked tea instead of coffee in the mornings. He learned that after many years of hanging out with Sean. So he set up the coffeemaker for himself and put on the kettle for Emma before beginning to make breakfast.

Noah was just about finished making breakfast when the sound of the bathroom door closing reached him. Closing his eyes, he again told himself everything would be all right.

Pouring himself a cup of coffee, he put his cup and everything out for Emma's tea on the dining room table.

Back in the kitchen, Noah was plating their food and stopped cold when Emma came in wearing just his t-shirt. He practically swallowed his tongue. So that was how she wanted to deal with this.

Damn, she looked good!

His shirt hung just above her knees. Her hair tousled. As though she ran her fingers through the short length to try to force it into some sort of order, after all the times he sank his fingers in it to grasp her head as they kissed. And now he was thinking about all the times they turned to each other in the night.

Down, go down! It was the only thing he thought of at that moment. It wasn't the time for more sex with Emma. Now he needed to convince his little head to think the same as the one sitting above his shoulders.

"Oh! Thanks for making breakfast. I'm starving! I really worked up an appetite last night," she said as she winked at him.

Narrowing his eyes at her, Noah asked, "No hangover this morning?"

"Nope. I feel fine. How about you?" she asked.

"Nothing some acetaminophen and coffee can't fix," he said dryly.

Emma and Noah sat down to eat breakfast. He had to say something about not using a condom during the many times they turned to each other in the night.

He may have been drunk enough to forget to use a condom, but he wasn't drunk enough to forget how Emma looked as she climaxed. Her head thrown back, her mouth open, screaming his name over and over again. It was heady stuff for him to remember and made him want to do it all over again.

If only he didn't need to go into work today. He'd have her back in his bed for a repeat of everything they did last night.

With condoms this time.

He observed as she doctored her tea. Dipping the tea bag in and out of the water several times before squeezing it out with the spoon and laying the bag on the side of the plate. She dropped in a couple of teaspoons of sugar, then swirled a splash of milk in before taking a sip.

Even making her tea was sexy. It didn't really help his self-control. Or lack of it.

Waiting for her to take a bite of her bacon, he figured this was as good a time as any to tell her what happened.

"We didn't use a condom last night. At all," he announced before shoving his own bacon slice into his mouth. It was the only way to prevent his babbling about the mistake.

Instead, he slowly chewed the crunchy bacon and waited for her response.

10

Emma jerked her head up to look at him with those words. Shit! She didn't even think about a condom during the many times they turned to each other in the night. He had her so tied up in knots and blissed out on pleasure that the thought hadn't even crossed her mind.

Of course, she was also drunk. So if she wasn't thinking much because of pleasure, she certainly also had a hard time connecting any kind of dots with as much alcohol as she had in her body. If it were anyone other than Noah, she'd be concerned about any diseases that may have been transmitted. But it was Noah, so she wasn't worried.

She trusted him completely.

"No worries. I'm on the pill," she said as she witnessed his whole body relax. She always made sure she was safe from getting pregnant. Just because she never slept with anyone without a condom—present company excluded—didn't mean she wasn't aware they sometimes broke. The last thing she needed right now was to become pregnant. So she always protected herself.

"Good. That's good," he said before tucking into his food once more.

Sitting at Noah's table, eating breakfast, her mind wandered back to last night. It was the best sex of her life. And in no way did Emma want to stop doing it either. So of course she walked out of the bedroom and into the kitchen wearing Noah's t-shirt —and only his t-shirt. She wanted to see if the attraction she was still feeling for him was reciprocated.

Besides, she'd do just about anything to keep him interested after a night like last night. The more they continued having sex, meant the longer she had orgasms she didn't need to give herself after the idiots she usually went out with finished before her, then fell asleep without making sure she was satisfied. Not with Noah. He made sure she came multiple times before and during sex.

But she also knew a couple of things that might keep them from continuing their activities with each other.

First, Noah was probably freaking out over sleeping with her, worried about what would happen when Sean found out. Her brother was one of Noah's best friends, and they did everything together when they weren't working.

Second, if Sean found out, he was going to flip!

But she was a grown woman. She may live with her brother, but not because she needed someone to watch out for her or anything. It made sense for them to live together because they had always been close, they were both single, both artists with strange hours, and they both wanted to go out on their own, but couldn't afford to rent or buy a nice place on their artist earnings.

Her brother, on the other hand, did have some kind of misguided thoughts about having to take care of Emma and protect her. Ridiculous as it was. He didn't seem to have a problem with her sleeping with men he didn't know, but one of his best friends? Yeah, he'd have a problem with that.

So yes, Sean was going to flip out! One thing at a time though. All they needed to do was make sure Sean didn't find out, and they would work this chemistry out of their systems, then go their separate ways, remaining friends in the end. No problem, right?

"You know, we can't tell your brother. Or anyone, actually. Umm...what I mean is that no one can know that we had sex last night," he stammered out.

"I agree. So what do we tell everyone?" she began. "What did you tell them before you left?"

"I told them I was getting my med kit to check your burn, then heading home after I was done since I had an early morning at the hospital," he replied.

"Okay. That's good. I can work with that. If anyone asks me where I went, I'll just say I saw you leaving for the med kit and decided it was easier to go with you. After you finished checking my burn, I left to go hang out with some friends." Emma thought that wouldn't be unlike her. She sometimes liked to hang out with friends who were still down in Orlando. And she would regularly stay the night.

"And I'll say you came here, I checked your burn, and then you left. Best to keep it simple," he said.

"Again, I agree." This was exactly what she wanted. Someone who was good in bed, was trustworthy, and was friends with to have a blistering secret affair until they burned themselves out. Then they would move on to something—or someone in this case—else. Now to just find out if he would be all right with it.

Clearing her throat, she decided to proposition him when he looked up. "So, um, I have an idea." Damn, why was this so hard?

"What kind of idea?" he asked suspiciously.

Pull on your big girl panties, Emma—not that she was wearing any right now—you can do this. She normally wasn't someone who was outspoken in situations like this. She liked when others took charge and she just sort of followed along. Emma loved going out to the clubs and bars with Ryleigh because she was so outgoing and outspoken when it came to people they didn't know. Emma just sort of reaped the benefits of that. But this was Noah, and she knew him very well. More now than she did before.

"I think we should keep having sex and not tell anyone," she blurted out.

Coffee sprayed over the table. Maybe she should have waited. Noah had just taken a big gulp of his coffee to wash down the meal he was eating, so maybe not the best timing.

"Umm...what!?" he spluttered as he mopped up some of the coffee on the table.

"Just what I said. It was good, right? So we should keep on doing it. Without telling anyone, of course." For some reason, the more nervous he appeared, the more confident she felt. This wasn't something he was taking lightly. She sure wasn't, and it was nice to know he was as serious as she was about making the right decision. "So what do you say?"

Eyeing her warily, Noah sat back in his chair. "I need to go to the hospital for surgery this morning, then I'm at the clinic all afternoon. Let's take a day or two to think about it, okay?" he asked.

"Deal. I need to go home and then head to my workshop. Thanks for everything. I'll just change into my own clothes and call for a ride home," Emma said as she got up from the chair, grabbing her plate and teacup to bring into the kitchen on her way.

"I can bring you home, Emma," he said softly.

"Better if you don't."

At his nod, she turned and finished her task before walking back to the bedroom to change.

11

Later that day, Noah decided he would think about what he was going to do with Emma after work. Even with that decision, it was hard not to think about last night or this morning. Everything he imagined being with her would be like was blown out of the water. Sex with Emma was better than anything he had ever experienced before, and it was all because of her.

She didn't know it, but Emma was exactly who he wanted in his life whenever he thought of his future with a wife and family. It didn't hurt that the sex was the best he'd ever had with anyone. Probably because he had been secretly in love with her for so long.

Random thoughts of the night before flashed into his head throughout the morning, despite having to concentrate during the surgery he performed at the hospital. Luckily, it was a procedure he could do in his sleep, because when he was done, he barely remembered doing it.

Obviously, they couldn't be together again, right?

Her brother would be a problem to deal with if they did. But Emma didn't want a relationship with him. No...she wanted to have a fling until it burned out. No way that was going to happen.

Noah would never get enough of her. He figured he needed another fifty years or more to make sure. If only Emma wanted an actual relationship. He may need to let her go if she wouldn't go for it. But damn, he'd been attracted to her it seemed like forever, and now that they'd slept together, that attraction was stronger. He felt more confused than ever about what to do.

Heading back to the clinic, Noah walked through the door into the reception area.

"Good afternoon, Allison," he greeted the front desk receptionist with a smile. Just because he was zoning out didn't mean he shouldn't be polite and happy. He did finally spend a wonderful night with the woman he had loved nearly all his adult life. Why not let his happiness show? He'd worry about the rest later.

"Hi, Noah. How'd the surgery go?" Allison asked, continuing to organize the files on her desk.

"It went well. No problems. What's my schedule like today?" he asked.

"You have three patients coming up in a few minutes. Sid asked me to let you know he'd like to see you in his office first when you came in," she explained.

"Okay. Thanks for letting me know. I'll go to him now." Well, that dimmed his smile and happiness a little. What would he want to see him about? Did this have something to do with one of his patients?

Maybe the surgery this morning didn't go as well as he thought. Noah knew he needed to pay more attention. He hoped he hadn't screwed anything up. He may be a seasoned doctor, but that didn't mean he didn't sometimes question his own abilities on occasion. He wanted his record at the hospital to reflect favorably on Dr. Mancera and the clinic. He didn't want his work at the hospital to cause any problems that would make the clinic and the other doctor look bad.

Noah wasn't a new doctor by any means, but he also hadn't been working for decades either. He understood that most thirty-year-old's were still finishing up their residencies, but he fast-tracked his education. He was always aware of what he wanted to do when he grew up. It made him work harder to accomplish his goals.

He always loved school and learning. Noah spent his high school years completing pre-med coursework toward his bachelor's degree, going as far as not taking any summers off. By the time he finished high school, he essentially had two semesters left to complete his degree.

Then he attended a three-year medical school program, which basically consolidated all four years of work into three. He spent four years in residency. There wasn't any way to shorten that time, and he wouldn't have wanted to. It was where he learned the most about being a doctor.

If he were honest, he most likely wouldn't be where he was now if it weren't for Dr. Sid Mancera. He told him when he went away to medical school that he'd hold a place for him at the clinic as soon as he finished his residency. Noah knew how lucky he was to have a position waiting for him so soon after residency. He also wanted to make himself more valuable, taking on a second residency at the local hospital in general surgery. Sid let him split his time between the hospital and the clinic whenever he needed to, saying it made him a bigger asset to the clinic.

Walking up to Dr. Mancera's office, Noah knocked on the door and opened it at the muted "come in" coming from the other side. "Hey, Sid. Allison said you wanted to see me?"

"Yes, shut the door and have a seat," the older man said.

Damn, this couldn't be good, could it? Stepping into the

room, he closed the door and took a seat on the chair opposite the other doctor's desk.

"I'm not going to beat around the bush. Neither one of us has the time to waste around here," the doctor began. "I want to retire and sell the clinic."

What! Dr. Mancera was going to sell the clinic? What would Noah do then? He supposed he could continue working at the clinic with whoever bought it. It was a risk because the new doctor might be an egotistical jerk or someone who didn't want to run the clinic in the same way as Sid. If that happened, he would need to find a new job at the hospital. The private practice in Riverview may be looking for another doctor.

But every option he thought about required more driving time or moving away from his hometown, his family, and Emma. Not that he would be much farther since Pine Grove and Riverview were literally right next door. Living in downtown Cypress Bay, though, would no longer be convenient if he had to take a new job elsewhere.

Noah was so wrapped up in his thoughts that he almost missed what the older doctor said next. "I want you to think about buying the clinic from me."

"You want me to buy the clinic?" Noah was in shock. How would he even begin to think about affording to buy the clinic? He didn't have that kind of money.

"I know you most likely can't afford it right now, but we can talk more about that later. Now we have patients waiting for us. Think about it and then we can talk later this week," Sid said as he walked out of his office with Noah, closing the door behind him.

The older doctor walked around the corner to his side of the clinic. Noah felt like he was in a trance. Dr. Mancera wanted him to buy the clinic? His whole body tightened, the stress over the decision he would need to make overcoming him, as he wondered if it were possible.

Deep in his thoughts, Noah casually acknowledged Leann —thank goodness she was all right after the incident with the man the other day—on his way to his side of the clinic where his patient rooms were located. Turning the corner, he ran straight into his nurse, Marcy.

"I'm sorry. Are you okay, Marcy?" He was a much bigger man than his nurse. The last thing he wanted to do was hurt her.

"Oh, I'm not sure. Maybe you could help me to the chair; I'm sure I'll be fine. Just shaken up a bit, I think," she said coyly.

"Sure, no problem. Do you need anything?" He needed to start paying attention to what he was doing and where he was going today. First it was the surgery at the hospital, and now just walking around the clinic he nearly knocked down his nurse.

"I'm fine, Noah, really. I just needed a moment. You have a patient in room two waiting for you. I'll just sit here for a moment more, then go check on the patient in room three," she told him.

"Okay, if you're sure. Let me know if you hurt anywhere or don't feel right and I'll take a look," he offered.

"I'm sure I'll be all right, but I will of course let you know if I need to," she reassured him.

Confident that everything was good with his nurse, Noah moved onto room two, entering after a knock to finish out his day.

12

Well...that was interesting, Emma thought as she sat back in the seat of the rideshare on her way home to change for the day.

Her attention switched to the rest of her day and what she'd do once she got home. She wanted to go into her workshop and work on some more of her pottery pieces. Several pieces were waiting to be fired, some in the glazing stage, and others ready to pack up for delivery to the store downtown. Not only did she always have work waiting for her, but she always thought better while working, too.

And now that she was away from Noah, she couldn't believe she had acted and said the things she did. Would Noah tell Sean what had happened? Doubtful. He didn't have a death wish, and Sean would kill him. So, that wasn't something she needed to worry about.

Would he pretend it never happened? Time would tell, but also doubtful. How he looked at her this morning told her she wouldn't be on her way home if he didn't need to go into surgery. Would he want to have sex with her again? That was

55

what she would prefer, but she was still shocked by how forward she was with Noah.

She had never acted like that before. Her personality was more laid-back and reserved, except with her family and closest friends. Sure, she liked to go out to clubs with her friends, at least until she used up her quota of socializing. But she wasn't one to go out on the dance floor much. Sitting at a table, talking with her friends was more her speed. She wasn't sure what got into her, but she did know she wanted more nights like the one she just spent with Noah.

The driver pulled into the driveway, where she completed her transaction and exited the car. As she entered the house, Sean came out of his workspace—he painted in the sunroom, which gave him the amount of light he needed, or so he said. Her brother did a double take when she came in the front door still wearing the clothes from the party.

His eyes narrowed at her as he looked her up and down. "I see you're finally slinking back in. Have fun with anyone we know?" he asked.

His narrowed eyes gave away that he was thinking about Noah. "No one you know."

"So it's just a coincidence that Noah was also missing from the rest of the party?" How dare he insinuate that Noah would take advantage of her in any way? Because that was what he was doing. Her brother still thought of her as a little girl he needed to protect. That he would think for one moment that Noah was someone who could take advantage of her, or that Emma needed protecting, then he had another thing coming.

"I did leave with Noah," she started, Sean glaring even more. "He was going to his apartment to get his medical kit and bring it back to the resort to check my burn. I saw him leaving after I went to the restroom and thought it was ridiculous for him to leave only to come back to the resort. So I went with him. But once he was done looking at my burn, I left and didn't feel like coming home. I met up with some friends in Orlando, and we went bar hopping. I had too much to drink and stayed the night at one of my friends. Not that it's any of your business," she sneered.

Sean snorted at that. Sure, it was okay for him to do the same, but when it was her, he started having problems with it. It might be time to sic their mother on him again. She'd set him straight. The last time he got too protective, their mother told him to stop smothering her. They'd already raised Emma to be a responsible adult; she didn't need Sean to continue.

"What's up with you and the nurse, anyway?" If it was okay for him to ask Emma about what she'd been up to, then she would do the same in return.

"None of your business," he said with a smirk, turning and walking back toward the sunroom.

"Seriously! Talk about double standards," Emma was pissed. That was just fine. See if she told him anything else anymore. The rat! She was an adult and didn't need to explain herself to her brother every time she went out. He wasn't her keeper, she thought. Walking into her room, she slammed the door behind her. Stripping off her clothes on her way to the bathroom to shower and change.

How dare he act as if she wasn't allowed to see whoever she wanted whenever she wanted? She wasn't a child, and he wasn't her father. Even if he was her father, that still wouldn't give him the right to tell her what to do or who she could date. If she wanted to sleep with all of his friends, she would! And there was nothing he could do about it!

Of course, she wasn't attracted to all of his friends. Just Noah. It would be weird thinking this way about any of Sean's other friends. Especially since most of them were also Kerrigans.

And another thing that pissed her off was that he felt he was allowed to ask her anything about her social life and expect an answer, yet wasn't bound by the same rules. Emma didn't want a play-by-play of his love life. Because, eww...that was gross. Besides, with her brother's exploits, she would be listening to them all day.

But she did want to have a relationship with her brother that included respect, and that was something she didn't feel like she was getting from him right now. Oh, she knew he respected her as a roommate and in her career, but he still treated her like a little kid in all other areas, and that was seriously starting to piss her off.

Needing to leave the house before she searched out her brother to tell him off—it wouldn't solve anything with him— Emma finished getting dressed, grabbing a banana and water from the kitchen before heading out the door.

She'd go into her workshop for a while this morning and work everything out, from Noah to Sean and back to Noah again. Hopefully, she would figure out what she was going to do with them both.

13

Noah stepped up to the door of the local bar, simply called The Bar. He shook his head every time he went to the place. The owner, Ben Carter, once told him his daughter Charli named it when she was eight, and he decided to just go with it. Now she was twelve and gave him grief about listening to her. Ben said he now kept it The Bar to rile his daughter up by telling everyone it was her idea.

The intensity of the sound increased as he opened the door. The sounds of multiple televisions playing whatever sporting events were going on, beer bottles clinking, and the mixture of voices consumed him as he walked in.

He was meeting up with Luke and Sean for a beer at the end of the day. Noah felt confused. He had so much going on in his head right now that he needed to talk to his brother and friend about it all. Of course, he couldn't talk to them about his feelings for Emma. That they spent the night together was absolutely the last thing he'd mention.

Luke would take one look at him and know. He wouldn't say anything, though. The last thing his brother would want to do was break up a fight between him and their friend at the local bar.

Noah thought being the sheriff was sometimes a pain in the ass. He would have no choice but to act instead of just letting Sean fight it all out of his system before moving on. And he didn't want to spend the night in a cell after being arrested by his twin, nor spend the next day at work all bruised and bandaged up. That wouldn't go over very well with the other doctors at the hospital. Dr. Mancera would probably rethink selling the clinic to him.

He also didn't want to cause any problems for Emma with her brother. If he found out, he'd go ballistic not only on him, but on her as well. Oh, he wouldn't hit her, but they would fight about it, and that would cause her distress he didn't want her to have to deal with.

But he would talk to them about his confusion over the offer Dr. Mancera made to him this afternoon. He was conflicted about whether it was something he wanted in his life or not.

Looking around, he didn't see either of them at a table, so he snagged one for them, ordering them a pitcher of beer and an order of loaded nachos. As a doctor, he knew he shouldn't eat all the crap he just ordered, but he was a guy first and loved this stuff.

Luke and Sean walked through the door just as the waitress dropped off their beer and three frosted mugs, telling him his order should be right out.

"Hey, I ordered us a pitcher of beer and some nachos," Noah said as a way of greeting as they sat down.

"Thanks. A beer sounds great right about now," Luke said.

"Same," Sean added.

They sat sipping their beer, relaxing after their long days, when the nachos and a stack of plates were delivered.

Noah was starving. He didn't have the opportunity to grab any lunch between patients. Ignoring the plates, he took a large chip loaded up with everything he thought a nacho should always have on top and shoved it into his mouth. He added a large gulp of beer to help wash it down.

"So, I hear you left the party with Emma," Sean spat out, glaring at him. Luke looked at Noah and raised his eyebrow. Noah almost choked on his beer and nachos, but caught himself before giving anything away. He was glad he and Emma had talked this morning at breakfast about the possibility of Sean confronting them. Luke most likely wouldn't believe him, but Noah would deal with him later.

Swallowing his food and beer, he was finally able to speak up without feeling as though it would all lodge itself in his throat. "I did leave the party with Emma. We went to my apartment, where I had my medical kit. I checked her burn because, as you know, she never takes care of them. When we were done, she left. Said something about meeting some friends," he explained flippantly, as though it didn't mean anything one way or another where she went off to.

"What did you do when she left?" Sean asked him, still looking suspicious.

"I was wiped, so I watched some TV and went to bed. I had an early morning of surgery this morning. Everything went well, but then something strange happened at the clinic today." Noah took the opportunity to change the subject. He wasn't comfortable talking about Emma to Sean. Besides, it wasn't any of his business. At least until it was. And right now it was most definitely not. But he did want some feedback about the clinic.

"What happened? Did you have another unruly patient? Why didn't you call?" Luke asked in succession.

"No, nothing like that," Noah replied. His brother was some sort of tough guy, but he was also someone who liked to look out for those he was close with, especially him since they were twins.

"So what's going on?" he asked.

"Dr. Mancera said he was ready to retire and wants me to buy the clinic," he told them.

"Can you afford to buy the clinic? That would cost a fortune," Sean said.

"No, I can't afford it. It will cost a fortune, and I don't have that kind of money. So that's one of the issues I'm facing with this offer. Sid told me not to worry about it, but I'm not sure I can," Noah admitted.

"You said that was one of the issues. What else is bothering you?" Luke asked, staring at him intently. Luke meant more than the clinic they were talking about, but his brother would just need to wait for anything else. No way was Noah going to talk to him about Emma. And if he was going to talk to him about her, Luke would need to just wait until Sean wasn't around.

"I'm also worried about being in charge of the clinic. It would be mine. I'd be the boss. I would call all the shots, but I would also be responsible for everything. It's a lot of work," he stated.

"Those are both valid concerns," Luke said.

"Dr. Mancera did say he'd work something out with you, so maybe the money part isn't that big of a deal," Sean pointed out.

"Maybe."

Noah still wasn't convinced that this was something he wanted. Did he want to be in charge of an entire clinic? Especially when it was the only one in Cypress Bay? He would be responsible for keeping it open. What if the clinic failed under his management? Then he needed to consider how much extra work it would be.

He would need to hire a manager. Technically, Allison already acted as one. Promoting her to manager and then hiring someone else to run the reception desk was an option. He'd also need another doctor for sure.

But he was getting ahead of himself.

Even if he did want to run the clinic, Noah didn't have the type of money needed to buy it from the older doctor. The cost of the equipment alone was astronomical, and he still had a ton of student loans to pay off. No, he wouldn't start making any plans until he heard what Sid had to say about it.

Decision made for now, Noah tuned back into whatever his brother and friend were talking about.

"So you and Noah's nurse..." Luke said, looking at Sean knowingly as he took a sip of beer.

"What? She's hot," Sean exclaimed.

"You are such a man whore," Luke said with a chuckle.

"She's something else all right," Noah agreed.

Though she didn't do it for him. She was always well put together and was a beautiful woman on the outside, but he thought something wasn't quite right inside. Her frequent acting was over the top, and he didn't believe that Sean couldn't see it for himself. Then again, he probably did, and that was why he went for her.

His friend wasn't one who wanted to settle down at all. Dating women who were far from serious was just the type he liked. That way, no one got hurt when he broke it off with them. It seemed as though he remained friends with all the women he had dated in Cypress Bay.

Of course, Sean had gone through almost everyone except Noah's cousins. They wouldn't date him if he were the last man alive. That was most likely why Emma was only friends with them and her girlfriends in Orlando. Sean hit on all of her other friends growing up. The bastard.

"You have something for her, Noah?" Sean asked.

"Not even if my life depended on it," he responded. There had only ever been one woman for him, and Emma was it. No one else would be right for him. If only she weren't his friend's sister.

14

"There you are! Did you get stuck working on a project in your workshop again?" the woman asked as Emma slid into the booth across from her.

Emma was meeting with her best friend, Ryleigh, for dinner at the local Mexican restaurant, El Sol Naciente. They tended to go to the downtown restaurant either together or to meet up with the other girls at least weekly or more. Usually she stuck with beer, but man, did she need a huge margarita tonight.

She couldn't stop thinking about Noah. At the same time, she couldn't believe she couldn't stop thinking about Noah. He'd been in her life for almost all of it...or at least since Sean, Noah, and Luke started hanging out in middle school. Emma never thought of Noah that way, and now, all of a sudden, she couldn't remove him from her mind.

Of course, the amazing sex was...well...amazing. Just the thought of last night had her clenching her thighs together to keep her from reliving the experience with Noah.

Ryleigh waved her hand in front of Emma's face. "Earth to Emma."

Snapping out of her memories, she stared at her friend as if she were just noticing her. "What put you into a trance? Does it have anything to do with a man?" Ryleigh asked, a knowing smirk on her face.

"Ummm...what?" Did everyone know she slept with Noah? That was the last thing she needed right now.

"That zoned-out and blissed look must have been put on your face from some really great sex. So who's the lucky guy?" Ryleigh asked.

Emma was relieved. No one knew about her and Noah. "It's no one you know. Just someone I met in Orlando. So have you been seeing anyone lately?" She redirected the question back toward her friend as quickly as possible. She couldn't have her stay on who she was seeing and be able to keep the fact she slept with Noah quiet.

Ryleigh snorted. "I wish. I'm too busy fixing and building things around the resort and town. Plus, no one wants to date me around here. They all look at me as one of the guys. Maybe your new guy has a friend he'd introduce to me."

Her friend did have a point. From the time Emma met Ryleigh and her sisters, she'd been the one who was the handiest. The only thing she wanted to do was build and fix things. And so she grew up doing just that, working with her father until she even outpaced him and went out on her own.

Now she was a one-woman building and fixing crew, who often contracted with others for larger projects. She was in a sense one of the guys wherever she went. They all worked with her and treated her as one of them. So she got what she was saying about no one wanting to date her in Cypress Bay. She'd need someone to move in who was new and didn't know her well for that to happen.

"I probably won't be seeing that guy anymore, but you're welcome to spend time with me in Orlando. You know some of my friends from down there, too. We can all go to a club. You're always dragging me to clubs, so you'd enjoy yourself. We should all meet up and have fun. Maybe you'll meet someone." Emma said.

Right after high school, she went to Orlando to join a pottery apprenticeship. She stayed during the week with a group of others who were also part of the apprenticeship program, then came back on the weekends to stay with her family.

It was a great opportunity and gave her the ability to learn more about creating ceramics, all the way to finished glazeware. She also didn't have a lot of money back then, so being able to use their kilns and wheels in her free time allowed her to work on her own projects.

These days she had her own equipment—thanks to help from family in the form of cash gifts—and didn't need to worry about traveling to Orlando to work. But sometimes she missed the camaraderie of those she had worked with at the pottery shop. While at other times, she was thankful she didn't need to share her space or equipment with anyone else.

"How come you didn't stay at the party last night? We were having a good time celebrating Oliver and Demi's engagement," Ryleigh said.

"I went with Noah to have him check my burn, then got a call from a friend and headed to Orlando," she replied. She didn't like lying to her friend, but the last thing she needed was for Ryleigh to find out what she did last night with him. She'd never stop asking for more details.

"Oh, to meet up with the guy. Of course. I'd blow off one of our parties for some really great sex if I had someone who didn't treat me like one of the guys. Though now that I think about it...Noah didn't come back to the party either," she said.

Emma swallowed hard. "Is that right? I wouldn't know whether he went back or not. Like I said, I left right after he checked my burn."

"Could you imagine what Sean would do if you did sleep with Noah? He's such a hypocrite, sleeping with practically every woman in town, then acting as though you should be chaste or something," her friend said.

"He's not the boss of me, and I told him so when I came home this morning, too," she told her friend.

"What! Did he get on your case this morning?" Ryleigh asked.

The two paused for a moment as their food and drinks were delivered. After tucking into the food and taking a healthy gulp of their margaritas, Emma told Ryleigh what had happened when she got back home that morning.

"That cad. Did you know he spent the entire party with the nurse from the clinic? They were hanging all over each other all night. Maybe they should have taken some of that back to the house or to a club rather than a family party. I wonder if that's why Noah decided not to come back? It must have been awkward for him to see his nurse outside of work," she went on.

"It was. He mentioned it when he pulled me away to look at my burn. He also figured I was uncomfortable, too. The last thing I want to do is watch my brother with one of his women. It's weird," she said.

"Well, I can drink to that!"

They clicked their glasses together, taking a large sip. Emma was happy that from that point forward Ryleigh switched their conversation to the projects she was working on and her sisters. She loved her friend, but wasn't comfortable having the attention on herself. Emma may like to meet up with friends in Orlando on occasion, but she was much less of a party girl than Ryleigh. And if she was honest, she knew her friend didn't go out as much as she used to either.

She was glad she had changed the subject because she didn't like to lie to Ryleigh. They had been best friends for so long, and they told each other everything. But Emma couldn't tell her anything about Noah. Even she didn't know what was going on between them. It was the best night of her life, and it may be the last one she ever had. She couldn't stop thinking about how he masterfully took control of her body and gave her more orgasms than she'd ever had with a man before.

Maybe it wouldn't be so bad to continue seeing him again. A secret affair wasn't a bad thing, right? And no one needed to find out. They'd burn out after a couple more times, then they'd go their separate ways and remain friends. She wondered what he would think about that. And was he even thinking about her at all? She hoped he was.

15

Sitting in his clinic office trying to complete paperwork on his last patients, Noah was having a hard time concentrating. And it was all his fault. He lied to his brother and best friend about Emma. And he couldn't stop thinking about being with her.

It was the best night of his life. He'd been in love with her...well, it seemed like it had been forever, but it wasn't that long. It was getting harder and harder not to shout it out to the world. Emma would kick his ass, though. She wanted to keep sleeping with him, but not tell anyone about it. She thought their chemistry would eventually burn out.

He needed a plan to convince her to keep seeing him for more than just sex.

A hand touched his shoulder, making him jump.

"Sorry, Noah. I've been trying to talk to you for a couple of minutes from the door, but you were so into your notes you must not have heard me," Allison stated.

"Yeah, I was just trying to get these done. Guess I was more involved than I thought," he fibbed to their intake specialist.

"You seem distracted lately, but I guess I would be too if Sid came to me with an offer to buy this place."

He wasn't sure if he was happy or not that the word had gone out in the clinic about the offer Dr. Mancera had made for him. Everyone was starting to treat him differently, as though he were already the boss. He didn't think Sid had said anything to anyone yet about him retiring, so that only meant one thing.

His friend Sean mentioned the offer to his new girlfriend, Marcy, who just happened to be his nurse.

She must have spread the word to everyone else because it was all everyone was talking about now. He would need to talk to Sean about it. He may be all right with everyone knowing to a point, but he wasn't thrilled about how that information got spread around.

What he talked about with his family and friends should not be spread around to the people he worked with, especially to one of his nurses—and a new one at that. It changed the whole dynamics of their working relationship.

He made a point of not hanging out with those he worked with. Noah didn't begrudge how others lived, but for him it made the difference in how he was able to work with them, and their ability to help his patients without any bias.

That was all gone to hell now because everyone thought he had something going on with Marcy. And no one seemed to believe him when he said he did not, that she was seeing his best friend. They all looked at him as if they comprehended the situation better than he did. And he didn't like it one bit.

He had enough on his mind between Sid wanting him to buy the clinic and Emma. The last thing he wanted to do was need to have a talk with Marcy—or heaven forbid Sean—to tell her to stop talking about him and making everyone think they were together when that wasn't the case.

Realizing he had zoned out again and hadn't answered Allison, Noah belatedly answered her. "Yeah, I have been a bit distracted lately. It's a lot to take in."

"I imagine it is."

"So what's the patient load look like today?" he asked, changing the subject. She handed him the day's files while going over each one, then left to go back up front when the bell on the door rang.

Quickly looking through the files, he had to get his head back into his work or he'd be backed up before he even started. Walking out of his office, he immediately saw the float nurse. Violet often worked for both him and Sid on the days their regular nurses had off. Today, she was working for him. He was grateful he didn't need to work with Marcy today.

Each nurse got two days off during the week, and they all worked five days per week. Marcy and Leann never took the same days off. Violet would cover for them on those days.

One day a week all three nurses were available, which made the day go extra smoothly as Violet would cover both doctors that day.

Also, the nurses rotated between working for him and working for Sid. That way they all learned how each doctor worked and saw all the patients in the clinic. It worked well and was something he planned to keep if he decided to buy the clinic.

Noah and Dr. Mancera would take a day off during the week, but often ended up working all seven days. There was always someone who needed to be seen at the clinic. He thought if he were to buy the place from Sid, he might like to have more time off and would need to hire two new doctors and another nurse.

Shaking off that thought, he needed to concentrate on his work. But he couldn't do that without first making sure Emma came over to his apartment again. Stepping off to the side of the hallway out of sight of where Violet was directing patients to the rooms, Noah pulled out his phone and texted Emma.

Noah: My place tonight? 7 pm. Come over hungry.

That was a start. He didn't know what would happen once she arrived, but he was planning on feeding her. He may want to keep having sex with her, but that wasn't at the top of his list. He simply wanted to spend time with her one-on-one without interruptions or anyone else around. He wanted to learn more about her...what she liked, what she didn't, more about her work.

And he hoped that by talking to her, Emma would open up more and be willing to have a relationship with him. A real one. Not a secret relationship he couldn't tell anyone about.

Sure, he was the one who initially said they had to keep their night a secret. Especially from her brother. But if he had the opportunity for a relationship with her, then he'd take it. That meant dealing with Sean, but Noah would handle him for a chance to spend his life with Emma. She was worth a million fists to the face, though he hoped it wouldn't come to that.

With plans made, Noah walked over to the first door, where his nurse brought the first patient, and knocked. It was time to get to work.

16

Emma again thought about this afternoon's text from Noah as she parked her car behind his building that evening. She wondered if when he said 'come over hungry' he meant for actual food or if it was a euphemism for sex. She'd prefer sex, but food would work. She hadn't eaten much for lunch that day.

Her work was finally moving along...to the point that she was almost too busy. Finding time to eat was often forgotten in the middle of her projects. So she wouldn't be opposed to a nice dinner. But if she thought he was looking for something other than a meal and sex, she was out of there. Emma didn't want a relationship with Noah. Her brother would kill him, and she didn't want to be responsible for that happening.

Emma walked up the back stairs to Noah's place and knocked on the door. Moments later, the door opened and Noah was pulling her inside, closing the door, leaning her against it, and kissing the hell out of her. Emma's thoughts were scattered the moment his lips touched hers. When this chemistry wore off, it would be like losing a piece of herself.

"Hello," Noah said when he stopped kissing her.

"Hi," she said, stepping away from him. While she loved his kisses, she wasn't comfortable enough with them yet. This was Noah after all. He was her brother's best friend and someone who had been in her life since she was a kid. The last thing she needed was for him to think she was okay with this. Even if she really didn't mind.

Noah frowned before smiling. "We should go eat. I got a couple of specials from the diner."

"I'm starving," Emma drawled, giving him a look telling him it was for more than food.

She followed him to the table, and they sat down to eat. Where she got this flirtatiousness, she'd never know. Emma was usually not very comfortable with it. But for some reason, being around Noah made flirting a lot easier.

It was as if their one night together opened something up within her whenever she was near him. She didn't know what to make of it, yet she figured it was due to the change from friends to lovers.

"So how was your day? Finish any interesting pieces?" he asked her as they ate.

"I actually have a lot of projects going on right now. I'm working on the stock for the store in town, but I'm also experimenting with making tiles, wall art, and some sculptures. Nothing's finished yet, though," she told him.

"That's terrific. Are you planning on seeing if the shop will carry these as well?"

"Not really. I'm just playing around with them," she said. She didn't think they were good enough to be sold. Or at least not yet. Instead, she wanted to test out different techniques and ideas to give herself something else to make besides bowls, cups, and the like. "How did your day go?"

"Well, I'm sure by now you've heard about Dr. Mancera asking me to buy the clinic," he said dryly.

He was asked to buy the clinic? "Why would I have heard about that?" she asked him. He seemed surprised by her question.

"You haven't? I thought for sure you would have, since it seems Sean already told everyone else," he said a little bitterly. Uh-oh. Was Noah having an issue with her brother?

"What did he do this time?" Her brother didn't seem to think before he acted or spoke. There was more than one moment when he had gotten himself in trouble over it. Mostly with women, but apparently he also screwed up with his friends on occasion.

"Nothing. I'm sure it was all a misunderstanding," he threw out before returning to his food.

"If it has anything to do with Sean, it probably wasn't a misunderstanding. You know he doesn't think before he plows right into things," she said.

"Well, this time he told everyone about the offer to buy the clinic, and now it seems the entire office knows about it and thinks I'm dating Marcy," he said wryly.

"What!" That was ridiculous. Why would her brother do that to Noah? "That doesn't make any sense. He's the one dating your nurse, right?" she asked.

"Supposedly. I can't think of anyone else other than Luke and Dr. Mancera who knew about the clinic offer. Sid wasn't going to say anything because he just sprung it on me. Luke wouldn't say a thing. He doesn't even talk to anyone here at the clinic. Sorry to say your brother is the only one left that I told," he said.

"No offense taken. I know how Sean is, but I still don't think he'd be one to spread you are dating the same woman he's dating," she countered. Her brother was a bit of a loose cannon when it came to keeping secrets, but he wasn't one to spread false information or make things up. She just couldn't see it as something Sean would do.

"I know. And that makes it even worse because that means he gave just enough information to another person, who then ran her mouth for her own benefit. And that pisses me off," Noah growled.

She had never seen Noah so mad before. If what he was saying was true, then he already knew who the person was spreading the lies about him.

"It has to be Marcy. Sean may have mentioned the offer to her on one of their dates, then she came to work and started spreading that information. Since I'm not one to start talking about personal stuff with those I work with, everyone assumed I'm dating her. How else would she know about the clinic offer? I'm pissed that she didn't disabuse anyone of that information."

"That sucks. What are you going to do?" she asked.

"I don't know. But I'm going to have a talk with Sean to get his girlfriend in line. I'll have my intake specialist keep an ear out at work and take control of the rumors," Noah said.

She thought Noah had a good plan, but wasn't so sure how it would go over with Sean to know everyone at the clinic thought his girlfriend was dating Noah. He may be a man whore, but he was exclusive with whoever he was dating until they were done.

As they finished up their dinner, Emma realized two things. First, how comfortable she was talking with Noah over a meal. And second, how date-like it felt. The last thing she wanted was for him to think they were dating. They were lovers and friends. That was it.

"You know...this feels a lot like a date rather than just

hooking up," she pointed out as Noah stood to clear the table, frowning at her words. "Not that I don't enjoy the food and spending time talking with you."

"What else would you enjoy instead?" he asked.

"You."

17

Thank goodness Emma still wanted to sleep with him, but how could he talk her into wanting him forever?

Forever?!? Was that really where he wanted this to go? Yes, he felt like he had loved her forever, but did that mean he wanted to get married? He had so much going on in his life. The clinic and his hospital rotations took up a lot of his time. And now Dr. Mancera wanted him to buy the clinic, taking over as the owner and all the responsibilities that went along with it. Talk about a lot of work! Would he be able to handle owning the clinic?

Then he needed to figure out what had been going on with his brother, Luke. He hadn't been acting like himself since coming home after serving in the military. He said nothing was going on and he was the same person he'd always been, just a little more disciplined after years in the Army. Yeah, right! It wasn't like he didn't come home on leave. Noah knew Luke was spouting bullshit. He was his twin, and something was wrong.

So yeah...he had a lot going on in his life.

The chemistry with Emma, buying the clinic, Luke's change in attitude, Sean's blabbermouth, Marcy spreading rumors.

And let's not forget that his parents kept on asking him when he was going to find a girl to marry and give them some grandchildren.

Because his male cousins found women, his parents now had it in their heads that Noah and Luke needed to follow suit.

He had to let it all go. Noah had Emma in his apartment all to himself. Something he didn't think would happen again. The first time was a fluke. This time was planned. He'd hoped she would want to sleep with him again, but he wasn't holding out any hope. Now here she was telling him she wanted him, so he would let the rest slide for right now and just concentrate on her. Emma said she wanted him so she'd have him.

Noah got up from the table and held out his hand to Emma. He didn't say anything as she took his hand, leading her to his bedroom.

"What about the food and dishes?" she asked.

They left it all on the table. The last thing he wanted to do was take the time to pick it all up. "I'll take care of it later," he said.

Once in his bedroom, Noah closed the door and led Emma to the side of his bed. He wasn't sure what he wanted to do first.

The first time he slept with her, it was fast. The intensity of finally being with her was overwhelming. He didn't know whether he would have another chance to be with her. But she came back to him.

So tonight he wanted something else. He couldn't make her love him back. Instead, he'd show her how he felt, pouring his entire being out for her to see. His only hope was that over time she'd understand everything he'd do for her, if only for a moment of being with her like this.

"Why are you staring at me like that?" she said, fidgeting where she stood.

"I'm not staring. I'm trying to figure out where to start," he explained.

He ran his hands over her shoulders and down her arms until he reached her wrists. Bracketing them, he lifted her arms and took a small step back, studying Emma. She was wearing a flirty sundress in black that floated to just above her knees, the cap sleeves resting a smidge past her shoulders, the front settled into a deep V highlighting her cleavage.

Looking further down, her legs looked smooth and tan. He remembered that she spent time by the lake whenever she was able to get away from her workshop during the summers, but he didn't know how often she went. He didn't go to their beach next to the family resort much at all anymore. He finally realized she wasn't wearing any shoes.

"Noah," she murmured.

"Where are your shoes?" he asked.

Her body was vibrating with anxious energy as he stood in front of her, staring. Noah wanted to throw her off a little.

She came into his apartment wanting to take charge of how things would go, but no way was he allowing it. He thought if it were up to her, they'd throw all their clothes off, have sex, and then she'd waltz out of his apartment as soon as they were done.

Nope. Not going to happen.

"What?"

"Your shoes. Did you come over without any?"

"Oh, um, no. I took them off at the door," she stuttered out.

How could he have missed that? Thinking back to when she first came into his apartment, he realized why he hadn't noticed. That's right. He was busy kissing her because he was so happy she was back.

Letting her wrists go, her arms dropped back down to her sides. "Take off your dress," he demanded, taking another step backwards, while beginning to unbutton his shirt.

It took a moment for her to comprehend what he was asking. The moment she did, Emma reached down to the hem of her dress and lifted it up her body and over her head, throwing it off to the side on the floor. Damn. She was perfect—standing in front of him in a black push-up bra and barely there black panties.

Now it was his turn to shift his mind back onto the task at hand. Shaking himself out of his stupor, he sidestepped out of her reach when she tried to help him unbutton his shirt.

"Lie down in the center of the bed," he told her as he continued undressing himself. She scooted herself onto the bed and into the middle, lying down with her head on his pillow.

He threw all his clothes onto the floor. His boxer briefs were the only piece of clothing left on. It was the only chance of making sure he went slow. Pulling open the side table drawer, Noah pulled out a condom and placed it on the side of the bed before settling himself over Emma on all fours.

"Hmmm...where shall I begin?" he wondered out loud. His gaze took her in from top to bottom and back up again. She was squirming so much it was amazing to him she didn't realize it.

"Noa..." she began until he cut her off, giving her a deep and slow kiss, tangling his tongue with hers in a slow mimic of sex.

She immediately relaxed under him when he dropped some of his weight down onto her, resting himself on his forearms and threading his fingers in her hair.

'I need to go slow, I need to go slow' was a mantra running through his head the entire time. He couldn't risk going too fast and not showing Emma how much he wanted and needed her in his life.

Slowly working his way down her body, Noah kissed and licked at her jawline, behind her ear, down her neck, nipping and licking the area where her neck met her shoulder. He raised his right hand to pull her bra strap off her shoulder, his lips following along, switching to do the same with his left hand.

Emma was squirming all over again, and he couldn't wait until he gave her an even better reason for her restless movements.

Reaching underneath her, Noah unhooked her bra, pulling it off and throwing it toward the floor. Using both hands, he cupped her breasts, plumping them up together. He pinched one of her nipples as he brought his head down to lick and suck on the other one. He loved how sensitive she was. She was writhing and moaning almost nonstop now. Noah wanted to spend more time on her breasts, but couldn't wait to move on.

As he moved down her body, kissing and licking as he went, his hands led the way, removing her panties with their descent. When he reached her apex, he had to repeat, *'go slow'* in his head all over again. Leaning between her legs, Noah held her open with his shoulders and hands.

"Noah, please," she said breathlessly.

"I'm just enjoying the view," he murmured.

"Less looking, more action."

She was trying to take control of the situation again, but that was the last thing he wanted to allow. And she was obviously still able to think, so he had to change that for sure.

Noah leaned down and breathed her in before running his tongue through her slit. Stopping at her clit, he let his tongue rest on it for a moment. Damn, she tasted good. As she started to move restlessly once more, he took her between his lips and thrashed his tongue over her again and again.

"Oh, yes! More, more, more!" she cried out.

This was something he could do. No way was he letting up on her now. He wanted her boneless by the time he was ready to slide into her. He slid one, then two fingers into her wet core. She was clenching his fingers tight, on the verge of coming hard.

"No...too...much," she gasped.

She may think this was too much, but he wasn't about to stop now. He was enjoying making her feel good and wanted her to come. Twisting his fingers, he found the area he was looking for and rubbed them over it, making her squeak. Knowing she was close, Noah sucked hard on her clit. Emma's whole body tightened and bowed up, his fingers being clenched hard inside her as she broke with a long groan before collapsing in a heap on the bed.

Satisfied he had done what he had set out to do, Noah slowly removed his fingers, licking them off as she viewed him through slitted and satiated eyes.

"Now the real fun can begin," he told her, reaching for the condom.

18

The next afternoon, Emma's thoughts repeatedly veered toward sex with Noah. Just thinking about what they did together in bed loosened her up after a long day working on her pottery.

Of course, they should have used up all the chemistry they had by now. She didn't want a relationship. She was too busy with her pottery, creating new products, and trying to come up with something new to allow her to do more with her pottery than only sell it in the local shops.

Not that she thought there was anything wrong with selling her pottery in the local shops. Both tourists and locals seemed to love what she made. And the shop owners, Sharlene especially, were wonderful people who helped her make a living with her pieces.

She made a decent living after all of her business expenses. It wouldn't buy her a fancy car or allow her to purchase a home without her brother. But her bills were paid, and she still had enough left over to buy an occasional meal out. Still, she always aspired for more.

Her brother, Sean, was making a name for himself with his

paintings. His agent, Leo, gave his work legitimacy, and now he had shows with his work in galleries nationwide. As a matter of fact, he had a show in Orlando coming up that he was getting ready for. He was always going back and forth to talk to the gallery owner and drop off another painting or two.

And what did she do with her artistry? Sold them in the local shops. Maybe she should do sculptures instead of pots and vases. Or maybe create a whole line of dishware that would appeal to buyers in the national market. Selling in the shops wouldn't be so bad if she were selling them nationwide.

But in order for it to work to her benefit, they would need to be limited editions. The last thing she wanted was to become an assembly line, churning out the same patterns over and over again. Sure, her workshop may be set up like an assembly line, but that didn't mean her pieces were all the same. It was only her process that was set up that way.

Emma knew where everything was in her shop and what needed to be done with it. So if she didn't feel like starting something new, she'd pick out a piece that needed to be fired in the kiln or glazed. Or if her stock was running low in the shops, then she could pack up some of what she had complete and bring them into town.

Anyway, that explained why she didn't have time for a relationship. Emma would be way too busy working on developing her new product line. She should just stop seeing Noah.

Noah with the body she loved to hold on to, the lips she loved to kiss...no, not love...she did not love anything about this. It was lust...an intense chemistry that should have burned out by now.

Yet what was wrong with seeing him in secret? To stop by now and then to have sex with him? No one needed to know. It didn't need to interrupt her work. She did feel amazing after a night with Noah.

Maybe telling him she wanted to have only sex with him and nothing else would be okay. And when their chemistry faded, then she would tell him she couldn't see him anymore.

So why did it all sound like it was wrong?

Maybe it was because Noah wasn't some random guy she picked up at a bar or club—not that she did that often. He was her brother's best friend. Her best friend's cousin. She grew up with him and the rest of his family. How would having sex with him and keeping it a secret affect their friendships? What happened if they couldn't stay friends once they were done? And most importantly, what happened if they couldn't keep it a secret?

The last thing she needed was to start a fight between her brother and Noah, or even between her and her brother. Not that it would be Sean's business. She'd told him over and over to stop butting into her private life. But he had some weird ideas in his head that it was his responsibility as her older brother to look out for her. Emma wouldn't stand for it. That didn't mean she would flaunt her relationship in his face either.

She really needed to talk with their mother again. Sean had to be reeled in and told to stop acting like he was her guardian. If he kept it up, she wasn't sure how it would affect their relationship.

Heaving out a huge sigh, Emma admitted she didn't know what to do. She wanted to keep seeing Noah until they decided they were done, but she also didn't want a relationship getting in the way of her work or life.

She also didn't want to strain her or Noah's relationship with Sean. She was very confused. Maybe she didn't need to do anything. Maybe she'd keep on seeing Noah when she wanted to sleep with him and play it all day-by-day. It wasn't ideal, or fair to Noah, but that was as much as she allowed herself to commit to him.

Emma had to get her head back into her work, think about

creating that new product line with her pottery. She had to let go of thinking about Noah all the time and concentrate more on her work if she wanted to expand her reach. Picking up her sketchbook, Emma began to sketch out her thoughts for a new project.

19

Later that night, Noah let Emma into his loft apartment. She was a bit curt with him when he called to ask her to come over tonight. She may have been busy working, but he also knew she still thought what was between them was some sort of chemistry that would eventually wear off.

He thought about Emma all day and decided he couldn't live his life without her. She made his life brighter and his long days feel shorter. Thinking about seeing her at the end of the day made the anticipation grow as he was moving from one room to another, making his rounds at the clinic.

He would just need to find a way to have her in it. Knowing how skittish Emma was about a relationship, he didn't want to give her a moment to think about anything except how wonderful they were together. So, as soon as she came into his apartment, Noah picked her up and carried her into his bedroom.

Emma let out an 'oomph' when he quickly grabbed her in his arms. "Noah! Let me down! What has gotten into you?"

Saying nothing, he deposited her on his bed and started to kiss her, while removing her clothes one piece at a time.

"I need you," he told Emma, removing his clothes. Sliding onto the bed over her, he pushed one finger inside her, checking to make sure she was wet. Satisfied she was, he thrust into her in one motion.

Emma cried out in pleasure, and Noah couldn't seem to get enough of her. He loved the feel of Emma under him and hoped he got to see her in his bed forever. She was so wet and tight around his cock. He never wanted to leave her body. But this was only one reason he loved being with her.

Unfortunately, it was the only one she allowed. She didn't want a relationship, though what she didn't realize was they were already in one. There was no doubt in his mind that they were dating. She was his, and he was hers.

"You feel so good, Emma. That's right, come on me. I can feel you tightening around me," he grunted, pistoning in and out of her body.

Moving his hand down, he rubbed his thumb over her clit in a circular motion.

"Aahhh. Yes!" she screamed. She went taut in his arms as she came with a moan.

As soon as her body began relaxing, it took two more strokes in and out of her before releasing a string of expletives while he came. Collapsing onto her, he rolled them over, making sure he stayed inside her as he settled her on top of him.

She was bonelessly draped over his body, her head tucked in the crook of his neck. Her breath was coming out in short, panting breaths. He was worn out as much as she was. It was one of the best sexual experiences he'd ever had. Caressing her hair and back as they recovered, he felt a wetness dripping down his balls. It took him a moment to realize what happened.

He didn't use a condom with Emma. Again. Shit, shit, shit.

This was not good. He needed to tell her, but he also didn't want to break up the relaxed feeling they had right now.

"Emma, sweetheart?"

"Mmmmm."

"I'm so sorry, but I forgot to use a condom," he told her apologetically.

"Mmmm...it's okay. I'm on the pill," she murmured half asleep.

Noah let out a relieved breath. "Good, I'm glad."

Holding her a little tighter against him as he caught his breath, his next thought was that he didn't want to wear a condom ever again when he was with her. He planned on showing her how great they would be together. To build a life together.

Since she was on the pill, he'd dispense with using condoms. As a doctor, he should be more cautious, knowing the pill wasn't a hundred percent effective, but this was Emma.

His Emma.

Noah didn't want anything between them any longer. He wanted to feel her without a condom between them. Maybe that made him one of those Neanderthal men who thought with their dicks instead of their brains, but he didn't care.

She was his, and he was hers.

Emma shifted a bit in his arms, causing him to slide out of her. They both groaned at no longer having him inside. A gush of wetness slid over him. He should be grossed out over having the mixture of their fluids dripping all over him, but he kind of liked it. The thought of Emma being uncomfortable, though, had him moving.

Keeping his arms around her, Noah swung his legs over the side of the bed and sat up. Emma quickly wound her arms and legs around his back at the sudden move. Standing up, he placed one hand on her bottom to hold her up. He liked that she didn't even make a big deal out of him moving other than to wrap around him. That gave him hope that she felt safe and protected with him.

Strolling into the attached bathroom, he removed one arm around her and opened the shower door, turning the shower on. When it was barely warm, Noah walked inside, keeping Emma away from the spray before gently encouraging her to drop her legs. Once her feet touched the shower floor, she lifted her head from his chest and looked at him.

Tucking a strand of hair behind her ear, he softly said, "Let's get cleaned up, then we can have some dinner."

"Okay, I'll scrub your back if you'll do mine," she replied cheekily.

"Only if I can scrub a few other areas on my way to your back," he said, smirking.

"Of course," she said with a smile.

They spent what felt like hours in the shower together, but was only about thirty minutes, washing each other, playing a little. He made her come again with his fingers and the water from the shower head. It was something he had never experienced with a woman before and hoped to do again with Emma.

Stepping out of the shower, they dried each other off before walking back into his bedroom and getting dressed. Together they went into his kitchen to eat the food he had prepared for dinner. It had to be reheated, but neither of them seemed to care.

Once they were seated, Noah thought he should say something about not using a condom again. She was half-asleep the last time, and he wanted to make sure she was really okay with him not using one.

"I'm sorry I forgot to use a condom tonight, Emma."

"Like I said, it's no big deal. I'm on the pill and clean. I've never been with anyone without a condom, so you don't have anything to worry about. Plus, you're a doctor. Pretty sure I can trust you're clean," she said nonchalantly.

"I'm clean. But just because someone is a doctor doesn't mean they are safe," he cautioned. He'd known way too many during medical school who didn't care and used their profession as a way to convince as many women into their beds as possible. That was never his style. He spent more time working and studying than trying to lure women into his bed. It just wasn't him. Of course, he'd been in love with Emma for a while now. He'd been with other women over the years, but the last few felt like he was cheating on her even though they hadn't ever been together until recently.

"I'm well aware," she said dryly. "But don't worry. I don't go sleeping around."

"I never thought you did," he said softly.

"So," she started after they had eaten in silence for a bit. "We can do this again then?" she asked tentatively.

"Yes."

"Okay...but we can't say anything to anyone. We have to keep it between ourselves. I don't want to get into it with Sean or have to explain how we aren't serious and are only sleeping with each other," she went on.

His heart sank a little at her words. He knew it wouldn't be easy for her to admit they were it for each other, but hearing she wanted to keep them a secret and that she didn't think they were serious was heartbreaking to him.

But he would take whatever she gave him for now. Hopefully, the more time they spent together, the more she would see they were made for each other.

"Fine, but we're exclusive. And we're ditching the condoms. If you need to get off your pills, let me know and we'll use them again," Noah insisted.

"No problem," she replied.

20

A couple of days later, Emma was leaving her room after changing from her workday. She was going over to Noah's apartment for the evening. She was enjoying the time she spent with him. Almost too much. The last thing she needed was a relationship. And yet she couldn't help but wonder what it would be like being in one with Noah.

He was very attractive...okay, who was she kidding? He was super-hot. He was muscular and sleek like a swimmer, and she had no idea how she managed to contain herself when she had her hands on him. He took his job seriously and knew she did the same, never making it seem as though his was more important than hers. Yes, his job was often more important, but he didn't make hers feel small or like a hobby.

She'd dated a dentist once, and he blew off her job as if she were playing around with Play-Doh rather than creating works of art. Nevertheless, one date was all he got.

Noah also made her feel special. He took care of her, not in a way of saying she couldn't take care of herself, but in the way that he cared for her and wanted to make sure she had everything she needed.

He fed her every night she went to his apartment. Sometimes it was takeout, and sometimes he cooked for her. Which was a good thing because her cooking skills ran to nothing more than boxed macaroni and cheese. Come to think of it, her brother wasn't much of a cook, either. It was amazing they'd survived as long as they had.

Of course, none of those things meant she was ready for a relationship. She was still neck-deep in her work, trying to come up with a new line of pottery she considered art rather than tableware.

The first few pieces were garbage and had to be scrapped. She wasn't satisfied with the outcome of anything she had been coming up with. In the meantime, she'd been cranking out more pieces for the shop downtown and was almost ready for another delivery. That would empty her warehouse some and leave more room for some of the bigger pieces she was planning on trying out.

Walking out of her room and closing the door, Emma saw Sean in the kitchen, making himself some coffee. He turned as she was getting ready to leave.

"You've been going out a lot lately. If I didn't know better, I'd think you were dating someone," Sean said.

"You could think that, but I want to spend more time with my friends. Not that it's any of your business," she responded.

"Those are the friends in Orlando?" he asked. "Emma?"

Thinking about what she and Noah might do tonight, Emma didn't realize Sean was talking to her at first.

"Hmmm?"

"Are you meeting your friends in Orlando again?"

"Yeah, I'm hanging out with my friends in Orlando," she said distractedly.

"Be careful," Sean told her.

Emma gave him a snort. "I'm always careful."

Leaving the house, she closed and locked the door behind

her. Getting into her car, she drove to Noah's, parking in the back as usual where her car wouldn't be seen from the road.

Noah was waiting for her at the top of the stairs and let her into his apartment. He greeted her with a quick kiss after closing the door, then led her to the table where he had dinner ready for them. Emma sat down while he plated up their food.

Other than the hellos they said to each other at the door, they didn't talk, and this gave her time to think about what was going on. Was he happy that she came over almost every night? He didn't say much when she came in, and he only gave her a quick kiss. Usually, he couldn't keep his hands off her when she came over. Sure they didn't always go straight into the bedroom. But he always made sure she knew how much he wanted her when she walked in the door.

Was he getting tired of their arrangement already?

Noah sat down after placing their plates on the table. Instead of immediately eating, he gave a little sigh and asked, "Are you okay?"

"I'm fine. Sean and I got into it before I left. He keeps on asking me where I'm going. I guess he noticed I've been going out a lot lately...more than I usually do," she replied with a shrug.

"What did you tell him?" he asked.

"I just told him I've been going to visit my friends in Orlando a lot more." Emma didn't want to talk about this anymore with him. It was what it was. Her social life was none of her brother's business, and the last thing she wanted him to know was about the time she spent with Noah.

Noah stared and it started to make her uncomfortable. "What?"

"I just wonder what would happen if you told Sean you were coming over to see me," he tentatively mentioned.

"Ummm...he'd come over and beat you up," she exclaimed. What the hell was he thinking? Of course, they couldn't tell

Sean. It would be a disaster, and she'd never hear the end of it. And Noah would be spending more time recovering in the hospital than working in it.

"How long will you continue to tell Sean you're out seeing friends when you're really seeing me?" he asked, blindsiding her.

Emma didn't know where all of this was coming from. She thought they had an agreement not to have a relationship and only see each other in secret until their chemistry burned out.

"Why are you trying to change the terms now? This was always supposed to be a way for us to burn off whatever chemistry we have going on here. We are not in a serious relationship. We're friends with benefits. I told you I wasn't interested in a relationship. I have too much going on, and I'm just not ready.

"Besides, can you imagine us as a couple? I mean, you're part of the founding family of Cypress Bay, a doctor who will soon be the owner of the clinic in town, and who also spends a lot of time working at the hospital. Can you honestly say you have time for a relationship? Or that you'd want one with me.

"I'm moody, live with my brother...who I'll remind you is your best friend...and I'm always working on my projects. When I get into the zone, I don't even answer my phone. I always have clay stuck under my nails, and my hands and clothes are often stained with it, too. I thought we agreed this would be for fun and nothing else. That it wouldn't change our friendship with each other or with others. Don't start talking as though it could be more," she pleaded with him.

The last thing she wanted right now was to stop seeing him. She enjoyed her time with Noah, and not just because of the sex. He was easy to talk to, and they shared a lot of similar beliefs. He cooked and always fed her delicious and healthy meals. And he took care of her, making sure she was protected walking to and from her car in the parking lot behind his building.

With the way he was staring at her now after her little speech—a little shell-shocked and if she wasn't mistaken, he looked hurt and resigned. She was worried this might be it. The end of their agreement. She would be sad, but she would pick herself up and continue on with her life. But then he surprised her with a smile.

"Of course. I just meant if you ever decide to have a relationship with someone, Sean will need to understand that you're an adult who can make your own decisions," he said suddenly, as though trying to convince himself more than her. The look in his eyes then changed as he stood, his gaze taking her in. "So what are you wearing under that dress?"

Emma was confused by Noah's sudden switch about her dress and what she was or wasn't wearing beneath it. Her tongue swiped along her lips as desire rose up inside of her just as quick as the change of topic. Going along with him, she stood up and started slowly walking backward toward the hallway leading to his bedroom.

"You'll need to remove it to find out," she said before turning and running to the room, Noah fast on her heels.

21

Noah's frustration was soon becoming apparent to himself in the last month. He thought he'd try to push Emma a little to test the waters to see what she thought about changing their status from friends with benefits to an exclusive relationship, where everyone was aware they were dating.

About once a week, he would ask how she viewed their relationship in the future, or what she thought Sean would say if he were told about their arrangement. Obviously, he needed to hold it in a little longer until Emma decided she wanted a more serious relationship with him. One that was out in the open for everyone to see.

He often confused her by quickly switching from a serious conversation to sex, but that was the only way Noah knew to keep her from thinking about them too much and then running away from him. If Emma didn't think about the fact that they were actually dating, then he would have more time to work on getting her interested in having a real relationship with him.

Noah laughed in his head. Of course, it wasn't a good plan,

but it was all he had right now. He was head over heels in love with her, and she either had no idea or she didn't want to acknowledge it.

He honestly didn't know what to do about it anymore. Did he continue to see her a few days a week at his apartment, feeding her a nice meal, making love with her before she left to go home? Did he push the issue of having a real and open relationship with her more, running the risk of losing her? Or did he give up, let her go and move on with his life?

He just didn't know if he had the courage to let her go. Would he be happy continuing on as her secret hookup? If it meant having her in his life, then he probably would say it was worth it.

At least until he was more settled and wanted to start a family. If she left him after he fell for her even more, imagining what it would be like to live with her full-time and have a family with her...it would devastate him.

Who was he kidding? He had already imagined all of that and more. Noah didn't know what to do with her anymore. That was the plain truth.

Sighing to himself, he got back to work on the last of his client notes. He wouldn't be seeing Emma tonight. It was the day she stayed late at her workshop. And he had another meeting about buying Dr. Mancera out of the clinic. The first couple of meetings went better than he expected. The older doctor had laid out some scenarios for Noah to be able to buy the clinic. They weren't ideal, but they were viable options.

The one that made the most sense had him coming up with financing from various sources, cobbling some from a bank loan and the rest from investors. Because of his student loans, he wouldn't be able to finance the entire amount through his bank.

So they came up with a few other sources of financing,

including borrowing some directly from Dr. Mancera and having his parents buy into the clinic as silent partners until the time came where he paid them back and bought them all out.

Noah's parents were real estate investors, so it made sense to consider them as a source of funding. They currently owned a lot of commercial and residential properties around the downtown and lake area, including the building where he had his apartment.

That was what the meeting today would be about—clarifying all the little details of where all the money would be coming from and the percentages needed to be borrowed by each of the investors, as well as their roles in the clinic as part owners until the day Noah would buy it back from them in full.

He already went to the bank to talk to them and got pre-approved for an amount that equaled about half of the clinic's asking price, but he also needed to take into consideration money needed to upgrade some of the equipment and hiring new doctors and nurses.

Finishing up his paperwork, Noah closed down his computer for the night.

"Hi, Noah. Heading out?"

He was startled for a moment by his nurse's remarks. Noah thought he was the last person left at the clinic. Sid had left about thirty minutes ago, as had the other nurses and Allison, who locked up behind herself.

"Marcy, what are you still doing here? I thought you left with the others," he said.

Noah was suspicious of her motives for still being at the clinic. Ever since the rumors about them started up, he thought she was the one behind them and telling everyone at the clinic about the possibility of him buying it. He didn't trust her one bit.

He had a talk with Sean about her, but he said it was

probably a misunderstanding. Yes, he had mentioned something about the clinic to her on one of their dates, though he didn't understand how that turned into Marcy and Noah dating. Sean had come by a couple of times since then to see her, which helped dispel those rumors. But he still didn't trust her at all.

"Oh, Sean was planning to pick me up, but he was running late, so I decided to stock up some of the patient rooms while I waited. He should be here soon," she explained.

"Okay. I'm on my way out, so why don't you grab your stuff. We can wait outside for Sean after I lock up," he said as he rolled his sleeves down his buttoned shirt, refastening the buttons at his wrists. No way was he leaving her alone at the clinic. Not that he would ever leave anyone alone after hours. She didn't have the key to the place. Only he, Sid, and Allison had access to the clinic.

"Sure. I'll just be one moment," she said, her eyes glued to his forearms as he worked on his shirt sleeves. A moment later she turned and left.

He watched her walk out of his office and down the hallway before grabbing the folders he would need for the meeting. Noah took a couple of minutes to look through them to make sure he had everything, then shoved them into his bag.

Walking out of his office, he turned and locked the door, then continued to the front of the clinic. He didn't see Marcy and was getting frustrated with her dawdling. He didn't have time to wait around for her, but he couldn't leave her inside the clinic, either. Just as he was about to go find her, she came out of the employee break room with her purse.

"Come on...let's go." He directed her out of the clinic and locked the door. When he turned, she was standing right in front of him, startling him again. Damn it! She needed to stop doing that!

Grabbing her arm, he directed her away from the clinic

door to a bench against the building. "Have a seat. I need to make a call," he told her.

He watched her sit down, then walked a short distance away. Pulling out his phone, he sent a quick text to Sean.

> Noah: Your girlfriend is waiting for you to pick her up. How long until you arrive?

He watched as the message changed to read, and the three dots started moving below it.

> Sean: If she's ready, I can leave now. Be there in 10.

> Noah: We'll be waiting outside for you.

He knew it! She lied about Sean running late. Marcy never called him to pick her up.

Noah would need to have another talk with his friend about his girlfriend. Something was up with her, and he didn't like it at all. He needed to keep an eye on her. He didn't know what her game was, but he was going to figure it out.

Not wanting to walk back over to where she was sitting, he called his parents office and told them he was waiting for Sean to come pick up his girlfriend and would be there soon. His father asked him what was going on, but he didn't want to talk about it with her sitting nearby. Instead, he told his father that he'd tell him more when he arrived.

Ten minutes later, Sean drove up and parked in front of the clinic. Noah gave him a look, telling his friend without words that they were going to talk soon about his girlfriend. Sean gave him a quick nod, then directed Marcy to his car and drove off.

Noah watched them go. He didn't know what his friend saw in her. He thought she was manipulative and didn't care about anyone but herself. So what was she playing at with him and Sean?

When they were out of sight, he walked the few blocks to his apartment building. One of the spaces below held the rental property office for his parents. Stepping inside, he put thoughts of Marcy and Sean out of his mind and walked to the conference room to start the meeting.

22

Five weeks and five days later and it was getting harder and harder for Emma to keep her relationship with Noah from her brother and others around them. Not that she was counting.

And yes, she now realized that she had been in a relationship with him all this time. A person couldn't be spending as much time with one person of the opposite sex without being related to them and not consider them to be in a relationship. Okay...maybe that wasn't entirely accurate, but in this case it fit.

She was in a relationship with Noah.

And it had been wonderful! She still wasn't comfortable going out with him in public or telling others about them, though. She was perfectly happy in her own little world of a secret relationship with Noah at his apartment. Emma went to his apartment a few nights per week. Any more than that, and Sean started getting suspicious.

They'd spend their time together having dinner, talking about their days, and generally just enjoying being near each other. They had actual adult conversations where he wanted to know what Emma was working on, and she commiserated with

Noah over a difficult patient or his nurse, Marcy. They also spoke about the clinic and what he was planning to do once he bought it.

Having actual dinnertime conversations was new and foreign to her.

She sometimes spoke about art with Sean, but it wasn't the same as talking about specific pieces she was working on, the new project she was thinking about creating, or how she felt to see her brother getting his work in galleries, while hers were sitting in a small town shop.

But what they did together after dinner was what she looked forward to the most. Making love with Noah was amazing. He was a generous and detailed lover who made sure she came several times. Her whole body felt alive when she was with him. And when they were done, Emma just wanted to curl up next to him and stay in his bed all night. It couldn't happen, though. She had to go home for the night so her brother wouldn't become too suspicious.

She found the perfect way to spend more time with him. Her plan to create a new product line was coming together, so she needed to spend more time in her workshop, so she often told Sean she was going to her shop to work.

Yes, most of the time she was really working, but often Noah came by for a quickie before she got back to work. He found time every once in a while to help her pack up her wares for the shop downtown, too.

Emma didn't know how he found the time. He was busier than she'd ever seen him between his patients at the clinic, scheduled surgeries at the hospital, and meetings about buying the clinic.

She wasn't about to complain. Especially since she benefited with multiple orgasms.

The only time that was becoming difficult was when Noah and Luke came over to watch games with Sean. Emma was getting so used to being around him that a couple of times she almost sat in his lap without thinking. Thank goodness she realized what she was doing before she did it and pretended to trip over him instead. Noah gave her a look that said she would pay for it later. And boy did he ever deliver the next night.

Tonight though was one of her nights to work in her workshop. Without any interruptions from Noah, Sean, or anyone else. She had a new piece she wanted to work on. It wasn't like anything she had created before. No bowls or vases this time.

This was an artistic project that, when finished, would become a large sculpture of Cypress Bay around Lake Tola. Emma had to create it in separate pieces. Once done, each piece would fit together to form the larger sculpture of the lake and surrounding shoreline.

Today, she was starting with sketching out the resort area around Lake Tola. It would show the lake, docks, and buildings around it. Her plan was to capture only what was directly around the lake rather than extending outward to the town. Though now that she thought about it, she pictured a large sculpture of the entire town. She'd need to work on one piece at a time to make it happen.

When it was done, maybe Emma would talk to Mayor Bainbridge about putting it in the town hall. They had a large rotunda in the center where her piece would fit nicely.

Happy with how the project concept was progressing, Emma sat down at the table in the center of her workshop and began sketching out the section she planned to start with first. She already had a rough sketch of the whole project, but now she wanted a sketch of each section drawn to scale. Emma would do this before she even began to work the clay.

It would take a long time to complete and would need to be worked on between her regular pottery work. Those paid the bills, after all. Once done though, she'd have a process to replicate it to other similar projects. Maybe she'd even create smaller versions of each section for the tourists to buy. The shops could market them as fitting together.

With a sigh, she admitted she always thought about what would sell with the tourists. Maybe that was why her work wasn't in galleries like Sean's paintings. Then again, maybe that wasn't such a bad thing. Sean was starting to complain about all the attention he was getting. She would hate that.

So perhaps creating art for the tourists was exactly where she wanted to stay after all.

Head down, Emma got to work, putting all thoughts of Noah and Sean out of her mind.

23

The next night, Noah's anticipation was rising at seeing Emma again. He loved that she had opened up around him more and acknowledged they were in an actual relationship. But he hated that she still wanted to keep it a secret and that he couldn't have her in his bed every night without worrying someone would comment about her not being at home.

Okay...Sean was the person Emma was the most concerned about. Noah wasn't too sure that his friend would care that he was seeing Emma. Sure, he'd be a bit pissed at first, but once he got over it, he would be happy that his best friend was in love with his sister. Noah was pretty sure anyway.

And okay again...Noah was fifty percent sure Sean would only break his nose and leave him with a black eye...maybe a split lip...before he would be okay with him dating his sister. Noah was all right with that. It was Emma who was not going along with the plan.

Maybe he should try again to see where Emma was in her head about them in a relationship. If she balked at his questioning, he'd redirect her into sex. It wasn't like it hadn't worked before. Though he had been laying off how much he pushed her lately.

At the knock on the door, Noah walked over to open it for Emma. "Hey, sweetheart, how is your new project coming along?" he asked with a quick kiss. He wanted desperately to give her a kiss that was more than a peck on her lips—one that expressed how much he loved her and was happy to see her— but he also knew they would never eat otherwise.

"It's going well. I finished up a second sketch today," she said.

"That's wonderful! I can't wait to see what you create," he said. Emma's work was always detailed, even for those pieces she said were so easy she created them in her sleep. Noah was always amazed by every piece he'd seen, and he wished she'd let him watch her work.

They walked straight to his table and sat down. He had already placed a couple of takeout containers on it, with plates and silverware. "What would you like to drink?"

"Just some water tonight," she replied.

"Sounds good. Be right back," he said. He went to the kitchen and filled a glass with water from his filtered system, placing a lemon wedge he had in the fridge on the edge of the glass. While he was in the fridge, he also grabbed a bottle of beer for himself. Picking up one in each hand, he left the kitchen and went back to the table, placing her glass in front of her before sitting down.

"Thanks," she said. "How is everything going with buying the clinic? You had a meeting last night, right?"

It was just starting to hit him that he was buying an entire medical clinic. He'd own the building, the equipment. He'd be responsible for all the employees and patients. And he would need to juggle it all with his work at the hospital and his personal life.

Noah was starting to panic a little at all of it, but he wasn't about to let Emma or anyone else know. On the inside, he may be on the verge of a nervous breakdown, yet on the outside, others would see him as confident and ready to take charge.

"It's going well. The meeting last night helped to solidify the money and roles of each investor-owner. I got a loan for half the cost to buy the clinic. Dr. Mancera will remain as a mentor and advisor, tapering off as I become more comfortable and as his portion of the clinic is reduced. He'll own about twenty-five percent of the clinic with part of the profits being paid out to him, reducing his ownership over the next five years.

"My parents will be silent investors of the remaining twenty-five percent. They've decided to remain investors for now, reinvesting their profits back into the clinic for the next five years, then they will also be slowly paid from the profits until I'm the sole owner. Well, the bank and I — I'll probably owe them for the next twenty or thirty years," he said.

It felt nice relaxing in his apartment, sharing a meal with Emma, and being able to talk about their day. He imagined every night being like this, where they came home from a day at work, greeted each other at the door, and then sat down for dinner to discuss how their day went. At some point, they may have children running around, making dinner even more interesting.

"Sounds like you have everything figured out then," she said.

"Yeah, but it's only the beginning. Once I take over, I'll be down a doctor, and I'll also need to reorganize some of the other staff, do some more hires, maybe even let one go," he said.

It was a concern how that would turn out. His plan was to hire at least one more doctor—maybe two—promote Allison to office manager, hire a new intake specialist to take her place, fire one of his nurses, and hire a few more. It was a lot to handle on top of learning how to run the whole clinic.

Noah would need those extra doctors since he would be splitting his time between seeing patients at the clinic, seeing patients at the hospital, and running the clinic. He still needed to have a conversation with Sid about the current situation with the nurses. Maybe he'd make some changes prior to the sale going through.

They ate the rest of their dinner in comfortable silence. Again, he thought about how to make this their life together every night. He had to talk to her again. Noah wanted her in his life, and not just for a few hours a couple of nights a week.

When they were done, Noah asked Emma if she would like to sit on the couch with him to talk. She looked at him strangely, her body held tight, as if she kept herself ready for a fight.

This was not their normal routine. Noah hated that changing it up put her on edge. Most nights they talked about their days while they ate, cleaned up the kitchen, then went directly to his bedroom, where he would try to convince her to stay for the night. It never worked, but he would keep on trying.

When they walked over to the couch, Noah directed her to sit next to him instead of pulling her onto his lap. He held onto her hand, shifting his body so they were facing each other as much as possible.

"Emma, I love that we've been seeing each other so much. I want our relationship to continue to grow. I admit that I've been falling for you for a long time now. But I want more than just seeing you a couple of times a week in secret. I want to start going out in public. Take you out on real dates. Tell Sean and my family that we're dating and..."

It quickly became apparent that Emma was not happy. Her whole face reflected her anger, that little spot between her narrowed eyes scrunched up. He couldn't stop now, but she didn't give him the chance.

"What the hell, Noah! No, no, no. I can't do it. You know why we need to keep it a secret. Sean won't take it well. He'd beat you to a pulp. And you know I'm not ready for more. But you keep on pushing me more and more," she yelled as she gathered her purse and keys up. "I need to go."

"Emma! Don't go. Let's talk about this," he pleaded.

But she was already out the door and running toward the stairs. He'd go after her if it weren't for the tears beginning to pool in her eyes. He hurt her, but she hurt him, too. She wouldn't even talk to him about it. Instead, she got angry and upset, then ran out on him.

He couldn't do this if she wouldn't trust him enough to sit and talk. It broke his heart to know she didn't trust him as much as he thought she did. Closing the door and locking it, Noah sat back down on his couch, resting his head on the back and closing his eyes. Damn...now he would need to start all over with her.

<h1 style="text-align:center">24</h1>

Emma ran out of the building and jumped into her car, slamming the door behind her.

How dare he bring up letting everyone know? Didn't he know that was the worst idea ever? No one would accept them together. Besides, they were just having a little fun. Eventually, they would have gone their own ways...ready to see other people. And he had a lot going on with the clinic. When did he think they'd be able to go out, anyway?

Starting her car, she drove home, the same thoughts running through her head over and over. Once home, her anger still hadn't dissipated. She entered the house, slamming the door shut, and stomped into the living room. Sean was on the couch watching a movie with his girlfriend, Marcy.

Sean looked up suddenly at her entrance. "Is everything all right? I thought you were in Orlando for the night," Sean said.

Emma stopped short. She forgot that Sean was having a date at home. She told Sean she was going to Orlando to spend the night with her friends. Now she had to come up with something fast to tell him, and she didn't want to do it in front of his date.

"Umm, yeah. My friends wanted to go somewhere I didn't want to go. So I decided to come home instead," Emma told her brother.

"Where'd they want to go that made you so uncomfortable?" he asked, ready to help her if she needed it. That was always how her brother was, ready to jump right in to save the day. But she wasn't a little kid anymore, and she didn't need him to save her or stand up for her.

Emma glanced at Marcy and back to Sean. "They just wanted to go to a pretty noisy club, and I was starting to get a headache, so I decided it was better to just come home and rest rather than risk making it worse with all the noise and lights."

"Is there anything I can help with?" Sean's girlfriend asked.

"No thanks. I'll just get something for my headache and rest for the night," she told her.

She still wasn't sure about her brother's girlfriend. It wasn't like him to be seeing someone for longer than a week or two. This one has been holding his attention more than usual, though Emma knew they didn't see each other a lot. That probably had something to do with it.

Sean wouldn't see anyone else while dating anyone, and yet he wasn't a choirboy either. He went through women like water. It was only a matter of time before this one went on her way like the others.

Sean was busy with a new painting, which was most likely the reason he hadn't been going out as much as he usually did. He would disappear into his work, and that would become his mistress. When he was frustrated with a project or couldn't think of what to paint next, then he was out almost every night...a serial dater.

Because her head really did start to hurt, Emma went to the kitchen, grabbed a water and then rooted in the cabinet for a painkiller. Downing two, she took the rest of her water with her into her bedroom and closed the door, leaning against it.

She still had a hard time believing Noah wanted to tell everyone they were dating. It would be a nightmare. Sean was already on her case about spending so much time out with her friends. What would he do if she told him she was dating his best friend?

No...that wasn't going to happen. Why did Noah want to make their relationship any more complicated than it already was? She just didn't understand why he was so adamant about wanting to tell everyone and going public. Emma thought they had an understanding.

Sure, she finally admitted they were in a relationship. But that didn't mean it had to be announced to everyone. Why couldn't he just be happy with how they were already doing things?

Maybe it was time to end it with Noah.

The thought had popped up in her head a million times over the last month. She never followed through with it, though. Spending time with Noah was amazing.

And if he was anyone other than her brother's best friend. Or her best friend's cousin. Or someone she grew up hanging around at the resort beach. Then maybe a real relationship was possible. Something public where they went out on dates, hung out with each other's friends and family as a couple. But that was not how it worked with her and Noah.

And it never would.

25

Noah was still in shock that Emma had left like that last night. He figured she wouldn't be happy with the way the conversation was going, but he never thought she would just leave. He didn't even have the chance to redirect her toward sex to divert her mind away from the conversation.

Shit! Now what was he going to do?

Noah knew that a relationship with Emma would work. He just needed to do everything possible to make Emma see it. Maybe if the problem of what others would think was taken away.

He'd solve the problem by going behind her back and telling her brother and his family about their relationship. Noah dismissed that thought almost immediately. Emma left just talking about it. She would never talk to him again if he said anything to Sean, or anyone else for that matter, especially behind her back. Noah would be cutting her out of his life forever if he ever did that.

Of course, what she didn't know was that his brother, Luke, already suspected something was going on between the two of them. He was not only very observant, but he was his twin.

Luke understood how Noah thought; they had the same facial expressions. His brother was able to read him like a book. Even so, he would never say anything to anyone else.

Luke tried to bring up Emma with Noah a couple of times over the last couple of weeks, but he quickly shut that down. He wasn't about to talk to anyone about his relationship with Emma until she finally gave in and admitted to him and herself that they were a couple. He was confident his brother wouldn't say anything to anyone else, so now it came back to getting her to come around.

If she'd even talk to him again.

Tonight though was guys' night. It was something Noah, Luke, Sean, his cousins, Simon and Oliver, and their friend, Joel, did about once a month. But now that two of the cousins were married and engaged-to-be-married, they had to coordinate it with their girls' night out. The place would change each time, and this month they were all meeting over at Sean's place.

Noah was hoping to catch Emma before she left for Oliver and Demi's home. Was she still mad at him? Was there a possibility of pulling her aside to talk to her under the guise of something medical?

Her burn was healed now, so the only other reason would be if she didn't look good. He didn't want her to be miserable over what had happened yesterday, but if it had given him the opportunity to talk to her, he'd take it.

Much to his dismay, she was already gone by the time he arrived. Not that he would have been able to talk to her with everyone around. He did want to see how she was doing, though.

Once they were all settled in the living room with plates of food and beer, the TV tuned in to a baseball game; they began talking about what had been going on in their lives.

If the girls were around to see them when they all got

together, they'd think they were the biggest gossips around. No one was immune to their turn to tell all or face the consequences of a stare-down.

"Joel, how're the boat tours going?" Simon asked. Noah was surprised he didn't already know. They were closest in proximity to each other considering Joel's boat tour company, Madris Boat and Lake Tours, was located at the edge of the resort property. They often did business together, with the resort having packages of boat tours and lake equipment rentals for its guests.

"It's going well. It's been a good summer," he replied. They continued a steady stream of info about business that he frankly zoned out on. He should probably listen since he was about to become a business owner himself, but he couldn't keep his mind off Emma and how she was doing.

"What's up with Aylin? She's been looking a little off lately and doesn't come down to the kitchen to grab something on her breaks like she used to," Oliver asked his brother.

"Yeah...there's a reason for that. We weren't going to say anything yet, but she's pregnant," Simon said.

"That's great. Congratulations! I saw her at the clinic the other day but had no idea why she was there. I was busy with patients and didn't have the chance to see if she was all right," Noah said.

"Aylin went to see Dr. Mancera at the clinic to make sure everything was good. Sorry, Noah, it's just too bloody weird having you look at my wife that way."

"I get it. It'd be weird for me, too," he said.

"She'll be going to an OB-GYN over at the hospital now that we know," Simon said.

Noah wasn't surprised she was pregnant. They spontaneously got married one day after walking near the courthouse. They were all surprised when they found out, and a little pissed off, but it was all good now.

"What's this I hear about you buying the clinic, Noah?" Simon asked, changing the subject.

He looked over at Simon and the surprised expressions of Oliver and Joel. Luke and Sean weren't surprised at all, of course, and just continued to eat, drink, and watch the game.

"How did you hear about it?" he asked his cousin.

"Aylin overheard someone mention it while she was at the clinic. You know she keeps her ears open, even when she doesn't feel well. Everything is fodder for her books," he said, giving a little chuckle.

"Figures. Yeah, Dr. Mancera wants to retire. We've worked out all the money stuff and roles of those who will be investing in it with me. Eventually, the investors will be paid off, and I'll own it with the bank. Of course, no one in the clinic except myself and Dr. Mancera was supposed to know about it, but somehow they all found out," he said, glaring at his friend, Sean.

"What! How was I supposed to know it was a secret?" Sean asked.

"Because I told you when I asked you and Luke for an opinion when I was first offered to buy it?" he asked sarcastically.

"Hey, I figured since it was about the clinic that surely she would have already known. It's not like it would have been kept a secret for long considering how few people work at the clinic," he pointed out.

"Who did he tell? This sounds juicy," Joel said.

"His girlfriend, who also happens to be my nurse," Noah replied. "By the way, why are you still dating her? I told you about the lie I caught her in."

Sean shrugged at him, taking another sip of his beer. "The only reason I'm still with her is because she's creative in bed," he said with a smirk. "Besides, you know me...I'm not serious about anyone. It will be a cold day in hell before I settle down like those two," he said, pointing to Simon and Oliver.

Noah shook his head at his friend. He had never seen Sean serious about anyone in his entire life. He couldn't wait until the time came that he was bitten by love.

"She does ask a lot of questions about you, though," he said, looking at Noah.

"Why would she ask questions about me?" he asked.

"Apparently, you keep your personal life to yourself so much at the clinic that no one knows you very well. I think they want to know more about the man who will be their new boss," Sean said.

Thinking about what his friend said, he understood why his girlfriend might be asking questions. Not that it would help. He was already thinking about replacing her as soon as possible. Noah didn't like how she lied to him and was hanging around the clinic after hours.

But there was more to it than that. He didn't know what it was. Something that he thought she was hiding didn't make him feel comfortable working with her at the clinic. Never mind that the times she did work, all Marcy ever did was a lot of complaining, making snide comments, or standing around gossiping.

He needed someone who was serious about the job. The last thing he needed was a nurse who caused more problems than helped.

Talk stopped for a moment while the player up to bat hit a home run, allowing three runners to score.

"These are good," Simon said to his brother, Oliver. "Planning on making them for the resort?"

"Yeah. I've been trying out some new recipes so I can update the menu a little," he replied. "Speaking about updates...there's a woman with a kid who'll be renting Demi's house soon."

This perked up his brother Luke, who had been ignoring most of the conversations, intent on watching the game. Noah knew he paid attention to everything that was being said, even if it didn't look like he was doing so. As the sheriff, he had his pulse on a lot of what was going on in the county and the town of Cypress Bay.

"Where's she coming from and what will she be doing here?" he asked.

"I think she's from Michigan? Wisconsin? Something like that. Demi has the paperwork. As for what she'll be doing...I don't know. Sounds like she's just taking a vacation," Oliver said.

"She has a kid. She'll be staying by herself, so where's her husband?" Luke asked.

"No bloody idea, mate. You'll need to wait like the rest of us and meet her when she gets here," Oliver said with a shrug.

Luke grunted at that before turning back to the game. Noah watched his brother with interest. Something else was going on with him, but his twin won't talk about whatever was bothering him. He'd just bide his time and wait until he had him alone to try to figure it out some more. It had to be something to do with his time in the Army that he was still carrying around with him. What it was though, he couldn't imagine.

26

At the house on the lake, Emma sat in Demi and Oliver's living room with Demi, Aylin, Ryleigh, Katia, Marinda, and Hailee. She didn't often hang out with the girls when they got together every once in a while to make margaritas and gossip about each other and others in town. But Ryleigh said she hadn't seen her in too long, so she insisted Emma come along.

Other than her best friend, she knew the other two triplets, Katia and Marinda, and their cousin, Hailee, pretty well. They hung out together every summer at the resort. She was always closer to Ryleigh, though.

She vaguely remembered Demi from when they were kids, though they'd hung out more since returning to Cypress Bay. Demi was friends with Katia more than the others, but seemed to spend most of her time sitting with her father than hanging out with the rest of them.

Looking back, Emma remembered Demi as always watching Oliver from wherever she was sitting. Guess there was a reason for that since they got together after Demi moved to Cypress Bay permanently after the death of her parents.

It turned out her parents had been murdered, and the

people responsible came after Demi. Then Emma found incriminating evidence when she and Katia helped her go through her parents' belongings. But now they were engaged to be married, and she moved into Oliver's house. Her parents' home was one house over. Emma wasn't sure what they were planning to do with it, though. Maybe sell it or rent it out.

Aylin was new to the group, so Emma knew her the least. She was an author who had come down to Cypress Bay from Philadelphia to finish up her book after a stalker got into her apartment. Her best friend, Angeline, thought it would be good for her to go somewhere new and warm until everything died down at home. Unfortunately, the stalker followed her to Florida, caused all kinds of problems, and was caught along with the local man the stalker convinced to help. Aylin was now married to another of Ryleigh's cousins, Simon, who ran the resort.

"A fresh batch of margaritas! Let the party begin!" Ryleigh shouted out as she walked into the living room from the kitchen with Demi. She held a tray of glasses filled with the slushy golden liquid.

Demi held another glass with a piece of pineapple speared on the rim. "And this one is for Aylin," she announced, handing it over to the woman.

"What makes that one so special?" Katia asked curiously.

"It's a virgin margarita," Demi said.

"What's the point of having a virgin margarita? The more tequila, the better," Katia said.

"Well, the point is that I can't drink any alcohol right now," Aylin said, pausing for a moment. "I'm pregnant."

The room was quiet for half a second before everyone started talking at once.

"You're pregnant?"

"Oh, my God! Congratulations, Aylin!"

"No kidding? That's amazing."

"Congrats."

"Thank you. We're pretty excited. But Simon's been hovering and nagging me every chance he gets. I'm trying to start a new book, and he's 'dropping in' five times a day with one excuse after another. He won't leave until he makes sure I've taken my vitamins, eaten lunch, my chair is comfortable enough, that I have enough water. And when he's not around, I'm fielding calls from Angeline asking the same thing. I swear, they are ganging up on me, and it's driving me crazy!"

"I'm surprised you were able to come tonight," Demi said wryly.

"Right? We weren't going to tell anyone else yet...I'm about twelve weeks along...but Simon said he'd only feel comfortable if he knew I was comfortable. So we agreed to tell everyone tonight."

"You know the only reason you could tell everyone tonight was because Simon can't keep quiet with the guys, right?" Demi asked.

"Yeah...they are bigger gossips than any woman," Ryleigh said.

"Talking about gossip," Aylin started, while everyone groaned. "What's up with your house, Demi? I heard something about you renting it out?"

"Yes. I rented it out to a woman who wanted to take a vacation with her son before school started. Her name is Gracie, and her son, Sebastian, is five-years-old. I don't know the whole story, but she's a single mother. When I asked about her husband, she said he was dead," Demi explained solemnly.

"That's so sad," Hailee said softly. Hailee often kept to herself and didn't speak out a lot. She was amazed they got her to come to girls' night. It wasn't that she didn't like her cousins or the other women, but she once told Emma that she often felt like she didn't fit in. Maybe it was because Hailee was more introverted than the rest of them, though she really didn't know for sure.

"It is. Oliver said he's going to make a bunch of meals for the two of them. We're going to stock the fridge and freezer, and I'll be going over to the house in the next couple of weeks to freshen the place up a bit, make it feel more comfortable for them."

"Speaking of places to stay...Marinda, how's your search for a new place going?" Ryleigh asked.

"It's not. I can't seem to find a place in my price range," Marinda said.

"You need a place to stay? What happened to your apartment?" Demi asked.

"They decided to remodel the entire place, one building at a time. Instead of letting us move into other units while the work is taking place, they filled up the open apartments before letting us know about the work. So we have to move out," she said.

"That sucks," Emma murmured.

"I wish I had known before I rented my place out. I would have let you move in there," Demi said.

"That's all right. I have some time to look. They gave us six months to find a place. I'm sure something will come up."

"What's up with Noah's nurse? I was over at his parents' office to pay the rent for the shop, and they were talking about something to do with her lying to him," Katia said.

"Isn't she dating your brother, Emma?" Ryleigh asked.

"For now. You know how he is. The king of short-term relationships," she responded.

"Well, I heard she has it bad for Noah," Ryleigh said.

"Where did you hear something like that?" she asked. Emma didn't like where this line of conversation was going at all. She may not be happy with Noah right now, but no way was Marcy going to be with him.

"I hear things while I'm around town fixing things. No one pays me any attention while I'm on a ladder or under a sink," she said with a shrug.

"It's not like Noah's going to date her, anyway. He's too busy running back and forth between the clinic and the hospital. And now that he's buying the clinic, his time will be even more limited. Though now that I think about it, the only way he could date someone would be if he worked with her. How else would he have time to actually spend with a woman?" Marinda said.

"True. It's not like he's a monk, but he doesn't exactly have time for more than a jump in the sack every once in a while," Ryleigh said.

"Crude," Katia scolded. "but true."

Emma was aware that Noah was busy, but he was taking time out of his nights to spend them with her. Or had before she walked out on him. Was that what she was to him? Someone to jump into the sack with every once in a while? That didn't sound or feel right to her. He was the one pushing for a more open relationship, one where everyone knew they were dating.

He may be busy, but he absolutely made the time to be with her—cooking her dinner or ordering takeout, sitting to watch a movie, talking about their day.

It hadn't even been a whole day yet, and she already missed him, she thought as she took another sip of her margarita. Scrunching up her nose, she looked at her drink. It didn't taste as good as usual to her for some reason. No one else seemed to have a problem with theirs as they all drank them down and poured another round from the pitcher.

Not wanting to continue drinking, she placed her glass down and made herself a plate of food instead. "So, Hailee, how are things going at the store?" she asked.

"They're good. But I did have an idea I wanted to ask you about," Hailee said.

"Me?" she asked.

"Yes, you. I was hoping to put some of your smaller items around the shop for sale. Would Sharlene be okay with it?"

Sharlene Walton was the owner of Artisan Crafts and Art, where Emma sold most of her pottery. The rest was sold online through her own website.

"Sharlene mostly goes for the mid-sized to larger items, so it shouldn't be a problem to sell smaller pottery in your book and tea shop. What kinds of things do you want?"

"Do you have any teacup sets? I thought I saw some on your website," she softly said.

"Yes, and I think I still have some I haven't put up on it yet, too. I could come by later in the week and bring them by. If you like them, we can price them out for sale," Emma said.

They spoke a little more about the logistics of creating more pieces for Hailee. Katia said it would be awesome if she featured some of Emma's items in her deli, too. And Ryleigh told them both she'd put in some more shelves in their shops to highlight the pottery that she brought in for them.

It was a little overwhelming that her friends wanted to sell her pottery in their shops. At the same time, she was happy to have such wonderful friends who would think about her pottery and how it fit in with their own businesses.

She felt truly humbled by their support. And yet, the guilt over not speaking up about Emma dating Noah weighed on her mind.

27

Emma flinched at the sharp knock on her door. "What!" she halfheartedly yelled as she lay in bed the next morning waiting for the nausea to go away.

What the hell did she eat last night at girls' night that was making her feel like crap now? She'd need to talk to the others and see if any of them were sick, too.

"Are you alive in there? You're usually already gone by now. Are you sleeping off a hangover after girls' night?" Sean asked while laughing.

"Ha-ha, you're a comedian, Sean. Now go away!" she yelled at the door.

Once her brother Sean went away, Emma breathed through her nose and exhaled through her mouth, trying to calm her stomach. Throwing up all over herself was the last thing she wanted to add this morning. Thinking she had it all under control, she sat up. The room spun, or maybe it was her head that was spinning. She must have sat up too fast.

Waiting until her head stopped spinning, she slowly got up off the bed to go to her bathroom. Halfway to the bathroom, the nausea hit her again full force, stopping her in her tracks. With one hand over her mouth and the other over her stomach, she ran to the bathroom. With her knees hitting the floor in front of the toilet, she barely made it before everything in her stomach rushed out into it.

Sitting back against the wall, it looked like she wouldn't be going to work today. She really must have food poisoning or something. Emma really didn't drink that much last night...barely anything, actually. It had to be the food. She felt bad about that because Oliver went all out to make sure they had a lot of delicious appetizers to munch on all night.

A little better after emptying her stomach, Emma wondered how long before her stomach revolted again if she continued to sit on her bathroom floor. She groaned as she got to her feet, walking over to the sink where she brushed her teeth and rinsed out her mouth.

Turning on the shower, she walked out of the bathroom and into her closet to grab some clothes for the day. Back in the bathroom, the steam rose from the shower, filling the room. She peeled off the t-shirt and sleep shorts, leaving them in a pile on the floor before stepping into the shower.

Thirty minutes later, a slight hollowness in her stomach was all that was left. Leaving her room, she walked into the kitchen to make herself some tea and find something bland to eat for breakfast...some oatmeal maybe? She filled the electric teapot, setting it on its base before turning it on.

On her way to the cabinet to grab a cup, Emma found a note from Sean on the kitchen counter saying he was off to Orlando to pick up supplies and drop off some paintings. She was glad she didn't need to deal with Sean this morning. Her stomach was starting to feel queasy again, and the last thing she wanted to do was verbally spar with Sean.

After making herself some tea and oatmeal, she sat down at the table and forced herself to take small bites and sips. As she ate and drank her tea, she started to feel a little better, but decided it might be best to stay home today, anyway. Just to make sure she didn't have a relapse.

Remembering she wanted to contact the others, Emma texted Ryleigh to find out if she was also sick or if she had heard about any of the other girls.

Emma: Got sick this morning. Maybe from the food? Are you good?

Ryleigh: I feel fine.

Emma: Hear anything from the others?

Ryleigh: Nope. Saw Marinda earlier, and she didn't say anything about being sick.

Emma: Okay, maybe something just didn't settle well with me then.

Ryleigh: Take it easy today. Let me know if you need anything.

Emma: Thanks, Ry. I'm sure I'll feel better later today.

That was strange. She was happy no one else was sick and there wasn't anything wrong with Oliver's food. But that still left her wondering why she was so nauseous this morning. She barely sipped the margarita, though she did eat a lot of the food. That must be it. She just ate too much, and her stomach was telling her not to be such a glutton. No worries, she'd take the day for herself and feel better tomorrow.

She was not feeling better. Over the next few days, Emma's stomach heaved every morning. Not that it was only in the mornings. She was nauseated on and off all day, but the mornings were the worst.

She didn't understand why what she first suspected was food poisoning—then figured was a case of eating too much—would make her so sick in the mornings, start tapering off throughout the day, then come back the next day.

Maybe it wasn't food poisoning or overindulgence. Maybe it was a stomach bug, or the flu? But those really shouldn't act that way either. She was very confused.

Maybe she had a tumor in her stomach. That must be it. She was dying and she didn't even know it was growing, waiting to make her sick and then let her keel over without warning. Yes, that must be it.

She sighed loudly. She really shouldn't let her imagination run wild. It would probably be better if she just called Noah. Though it grated inside to make the first move after telling him she was done.

Still, Emma didn't want to make a big deal out of her imagined illness by going to the clinic, only to find out in front of everyone she was a fool for thinking she had some fatal condition.

She remembered this was his one day off, so he wasn't at the clinic, and she didn't want to see the other doctor. Not that Allison would let her see Dr. Mancera anyway.

Emma trusted Noah. Even after their secret affair, she still felt more comfortable airing her concerns with him, despite the issues they were having right now. Especially if what was wrong with her turned out to be nothing.

Pulling out her phone, Emma texted Noah to see if he was willing to help.

> Emma: Been feeling sick, and it's not going away.

Noah: What are your symptoms?

They texted back and forth about what she was experiencing, along with why she didn't go to the clinic.

Noah: Can you come to my apartment in a bit?

Emma: Sure.

Noah: I need to run by the clinic to pick up some supplies first. Let yourself in if I'm not back.

Emma: Okay, thanks, Noah.

She vaguely wondered what it was he needed to pick up that he didn't already have. He practically had a whole clinic with a closet full of supplies in his apartment. Along with a bag of supplies, he kept with him everywhere he went—the engagement party being the one time he left it at home. He wasn't just a doctor when he was working. The man lived and breathed his profession. And it came in handy more than a few times when he had to be available to treat Aylin and Demi after their ordeals.

Shrugging that line of thought off, Emma got up out of bed carefully and got dressed. Who cared if she didn't take a shower this morning? It wasn't like he had never seen her looking far from her best before. And she felt like crap besides. It was taking all her energy to even get out of bed. She was so tired and just wanted to sleep another day away.

It felt like that was all she'd been doing for the last several days. She hadn't even been to her workshop. And her brother was sure she had the flu and was purposely staying away from her so he wouldn't catch anything. She couldn't blame him. She'd do the same.

Emma was appreciative, though, that Sean had been making sure she had food and drinks available. He made a bunch of chicken noodle soup—from a can—and put it into smaller containers for a quick microwave meal. And he bought her some lemon-lime soda, too. So, he wasn't a pain in the ass all the time. Only when she wasn't sick.

Leaving a note for her brother in case he came home while she was out, Emma grabbed her purse and car keys before walking out the door and locking it up behind her.

The drive was only about ten minutes, but it gave her some time to think more about her conversation with Noah that morning. He said something about picking up some tests to rule things out. What was it he was trying to rule out? Was she right? Did she have something more serious?

Okay...don't get yourself all worked up before you know what's going on, she told herself. It was bad enough that it was taking all the energy she had left just to drive to his apartment. Adding a touch of panic would do her no good.

Emma pulled into the parking lot behind Noah's building. His car was missing, so he must have driven over to the clinic. Luckily, he gave her a key to his apartment a couple of weeks ago. There were some weeknights she came over and he wasn't home from work yet. Entering his apartment without him wasn't new.

A wave of exhaustion along with a case of nausea hit her as she entered his apartment. Maybe she would go lie down in his room while she waited for him to return. Heading to his bedroom, she slipped off her shoes on her way down the hall, then entered the room. Sliding under the sheets of his bed, she settled in. The comforter and pillows smelled like Noah. She missed this, she thought, before drifting off to sleep.

28

Pulling up at the clinic, Noah parked the car and sat for a moment to collect himself. He thought he had figured out why Emma was sick, but he wasn't sure he was ready to cope with it.

Damn...it sounded like she was pregnant! He was definitely going to hell now...right after Sean killed him.

At the same time, he was happy about it, too. A baby! Did this mean they'd become a family? If the test came out positive, would she finally give in and allow them to have a public relationship?

Noah had wanted Emma for her entire adult life, it seemed. Sure, he didn't notice her much when they were kids, but she sure did grow up nice, and he'd been watching her for a while as she grew up even more.

Now they had been secretly spending time together. Oh, who was he kidding! They were fucking each other left and right whenever she snuck over to his apartment, or he spared a moment he didn't have to go to her workshop for a quick afternoon tryst.

Yes, they spent some time talking, sharing a meal. But they

were not dating each other out in the open like he wished they were. Maybe now—if his suspicions were correct—Emma would be more willing to come out into the open and tell their families about them.

Getting out of his car, he walked into the clinic, surprising Allison at the front desk. "Noah! What are you doing here on your day off? Don't you work enough?" she asked.

"I'm just here to grab some supplies I forgot to pick up on my way out yesterday," he explained. "Don't worry, I'm not here to work."

"Good. You work too much as it is. Once the sale goes through, you'll probably never leave," she said.

He nodded at her, knowing that was exactly what would happen. He made a note to himself to pull Allison aside later in the week to offer her the office manager position he was creating.

The clinic was always run on the small side, but now that he was going to be in charge and planning on hiring more doctors, he needed someone to run the office. He couldn't do it all by himself, and she knew every nook and cranny of the clinic. He planned on hiring a new intake specialist to take her place.

He walked down the hallway to the supply room and entered the unlocked room. They kept it unlocked during the day in case they needed to grab any supplies. That was Sid's decision. Noah didn't agree with it. He thought the door should always be locked until the time when something was needed. They had enough supplies in the individual rooms if they were needed in another room. And every evening before closing up, they resupplied each room. But even with the older doctor's rules, the door was always supposed to stay closed.

So why was it standing wide open now? He looked around but didn't see anyone. The nurses and Dr. Mancera must all be with patients. Maybe someone needed something and just forgot to close the door. Noah mentally shrugged. He really didn't have time to think about the reason for the open door right at the moment. He'd talk to everyone tomorrow and find out what happened.

Right now, he most likely had the woman he loved sitting in his apartment waiting for him. He grabbed the tests and a bottle of vitamins, put them in a bag, then walked out of the supply closet, closing the door behind him. On his way back home, he stopped by the store and picked up some crackers, water, and ginger ale. The rest of what he would need was already at his apartment.

When he arrived home, Emma's car was already parked in the lot behind the building. Taking the steps two at a time, he unlocked his door and went inside, expecting to find her in his kitchen or living room. Instead, the open area was empty.

"Emma?" he asked out loud.

Getting no response, he put his bags down in the kitchen and walked toward his bedroom. Her shoes were lying in the middle of the hallway. She must have gone into his bedroom to rest. He liked the thought of Emma being comfortable enough to go straight to his bed when she was feeling sick.

Heading for his bedroom, he opened the door and found her lying on her side under the covers, sound asleep. He slowly exited his room, leaving the door opened a crack. He went back into his kitchen and emptied out the grocery bags.

Pulling out a tray from one of the bottom cabinets, Noah snorted that he had finally found a reason to use it. His mother said she found it in the shop she worked in her spare time— like she had a lot of it, but she enjoyed being around people— and decided it was perfect for him and his apartment. He scoffed, saying he had no use for a serving tray. It wasn't like he had a lot of people over, and when his cousins, brother, and friends came to watch a game, the last thing he needed was to pull out a serving tray.

And now he would need to tell her she was right, he thought, shaking his head.

Well, he'd tell her when he got the go-ahead from Emma to tell everyone about their relationship. He hoped that would be soon.

He opened the box of crackers, took out a sleeve and put a stack of them on a plate. He poured a small glass of the soda, placing it on the tray with the crackers. Going to the fridge, he pulled out a bottle of water, opened another cabinet, grabbing a bag out of it, then grabbed a test he got from the clinic. He placed the rest on the tray and lifted it with both hands, carrying it down the hallway to his bedroom.

Nudging the door open with his shoulder, he entered his room. Emma was still asleep. He put the tray down on the table next to the bed before sitting next to where she was curled up.

"Emma, sweetheart, I need you to wake up," he said gently, while slightly shaking her shoulder.

He watched as she slowly came awake. It looked like she'd had a rough couple of days. It looked like she had swiftly put her hair up in a short ponytail, but since her hair wasn't very long, pieces were sticking out all over. Dark circles under her eyes indicated she hadn't gotten very much sleep over the last few days. And her skin was too pale.

"Hey, how are you feeling? No, don't try to sit up just yet," he told her when she tried to quickly move.

"Yeah...maybe not a good idea just yet," she said, looking a little wobbly.

"Let your stomach settle a bit. Here why don't you nibble on this," he said, reaching into the bag on the tray.

He watched her look at it with curiosity and distrust. "It's a ginger tablet. Chewing on it can help with some of the nausea," he explained to her.

Taking the tablet from his hand, she popped it into her mouth and slowly chewed, making a face at the taste.

"It's strong, but it'll help."

"Thanks. It's not that bad actually, but usually I have ginger mixed with other things like a stir fry or blended into a smoothie," she said.

"Think you can sit up now?" he asked.

"I think so," she said as she slowly sat up. He helped her with the pillows, putting them behind her to support her against the headboard. "I'm sorry for falling asleep in your bed."

"Don't be. I like having you in my bed," he said as he turned away from her. He was having a hard time looking at her in his bed. All Noah wanted to do was dishevel her more, but in a way that was fun for both of them. But he couldn't do that right now. She was sick, so he had to take care of her.

He handed her the bottle of water first. He needed her to be hydrated before giving her the soda to sip on. The ginger tablet should help with the nausea, but her stomach may still feel a little wobbly for a while. "Here, drink this. When you're done, you can go into the bathroom and pee on this."

Picking up the box on the tray, he opened the pregnancy test, pulling out the stick inside.

"Don't you think that's overkill? I probably have the stomach flu or something," she said nervously, looking at the stick in his hand.

He knew this would be hard for her, but he was going to be with her all the way. And not just because she might be carrying his child. He loved her and would be by her side to support her even if she weren't pregnant and did have the stomach flu.

"Let's rule this out. If it comes back negative, then we'll know it's probably the stomach flu or something else. Now drink your water, but slowly. I don't want you to throw it all back up again."

Emma looked so resigned, wilting at his words, he almost told her to go back to sleep. But she picked up the bottle and slowly drank the water down. When she was done, she held out her hand. He placed the pregnancy test in her hand and silently helped her sit up on the side of the bed. Settling herself, she took a deep breath, got up off the bed, and walked to the bathroom, closing herself inside.

While he waited, Noah made up the bed, took the empty water bottle to the kitchen, got a new bottle of water, and returned to the bedroom. She still hadn't come out. So he paced back and forth in front of the bathroom door.

After waiting a bit, Noah realized she should have been done by now. He stopped in front of the bathroom and knocked on the door.

"Emma," he gently said her name.

With no response, he opened the door, thankful she hadn't locked him out. Emma was sitting on the closed toilet seat staring at the test in her hand. Walking up to her, he kneeled in front of her and gently took the test out of the hand gripping it.

Emma looked up at him and said, "I'm pregnant."

29

Emma couldn't believe she was pregnant. It had never even occurred to her. They were always careful.

She then thought back to the first time they had been together. Then there was that one other time they didn't use a condom either.

Shit, shit, shit!

If she thought about it, she might have taken her birth control pills late or missed them altogether on occasion. It was hard to remember when she was in a rush to get to the workshop.

In front of her, Noah smiled, his eyes reflecting understanding and happiness as he looked down at her.

"What are we going to do?" she asked him.

"We are going to take one day at a time, sweetheart. But in the meantime," Noah gently grabbed her hands and helped her to stand, "let's get you comfortable and feeling better."

"I'm already feeling better. I'm just a little unnerved about all this," she told him.

"Do you want to go out on the couch or stay in bed?" he asked her.

She was physically better. Her morning sickness—now that she knew what it was—was worse in the mornings, sometimes going into the afternoons. But the ginger tablet helped, as did being able to keep down the water.

She was so tired, though. Maybe a nap wouldn't be too bad, though she didn't want to sleep her whole day away. She'd done that for the last several days, and she felt worse because of it. Emma would have preferred hanging out on her own couch at home, but that would have caused too many questions with her brother. And that was the last thing she needed.

Especially now that she knew she was pregnant. He would go ballistic. And once he found out she was pregnant and that Noah was the father. Even worse! She had to keep this to herself. She wasn't ready to deal with Sean. Or her relationship with Noah, for that matter. Emma wanted to concentrate only on making her stomach not want to hurl every time she moved.

The rest would need to wait until later.

"How about the couch? I've been holed up in my room for the last couple of days. I'd like not to be tucked away for a bit," she answered.

"Okay, think you can make it there on your own?" he asked.

"Yes, I'll be fine," she said a little curtly.

Emma immediately regretted the sharp bite in her voice. Noah was helping her, and here she was sniping at him for it.

"I'll go grab the stuff from the bedroom and bring it in to you while you make yourself comfortable on the couch," he said, walking toward his bedroom.

She made her way to the living room, taking the blanket on the back of the couch, before sitting down in the corner. His couch was perfect. It was L-shaped and wide, allowing her to fit in the corner and stretch out her legs. Throwing the blanket over herself, she settled the pillows behind her back and relaxed into the couch.

"Here you go," Noah said, putting the tray down beside her. "Would you like anything else?"

"I'm good for now. Thank you, Noah," she said, much calmer now that she was more relaxed.

He gave her a smile and said, "I'll be right back."

She watched him walk into the kitchen and pull a bottle out of a bag that was sitting on the counter. Opening the bottle, he pulled off the safety covering and shook out what was in the bottle into his hand. Replacing the cap, he left the bottle on the counter and opened the fridge, pulling out a water bottle. He walked back to her and placed the pill on the tray, then twisted the cap off the bottle. Picking up the pill again, he handed it to her.

"Here, you need to start taking prenatal vitamins."

She took the pill out of his hand and popped it into her mouth, drinking some of the water he then handed to her to wash it down. It may not have fully sunk in yet that she was pregnant, but she wasn't about to discount what Noah said about her health. He was a doctor after all, and from what she had experienced, a good one at that.

"Now that we know you are pregnant, there are a few other things you should pay more attention to, like staying away from the ovens in your workshop."

"There is no way I'm stopping my work, and that includes working with the ovens. But I will take the prenatal vitamins and rest more. I'll be extra careful, and if I feel off, I'll take a break. But I will not stop working. Just because you're the kid's father doesn't mean you get to tell me what to do. I'll listen to you about the medical stuff, but that's all," she said resolutely.

"Fine, but you'll do everything I tell you to do that keeps you both healthy," he said.

"I agree. But I don't want to say anything to anyone just yet. Can we keep this a secret between us for now? I can't handle having to deal with being sick and my brother at the same time."

Noah's lips pinched together in frustration before relaxing once again in a small smile. "I don't like it. But we can keep it a secret for now. Most couples don't say anything until after the first trimester, anyway."

She watched him run a hand through his hair, knowing he didn't like that she wanted to keep not only the pregnancy a secret but also the fact that he was the father. She truly couldn't deal with any of it.

She was pregnant!

And that was enough to think about for now. As for what she was going to do in the future about it and Noah, Emma wasn't prepared to delve into it yet. She was just too tired to think about anything else right now.

Sinking down onto the couch, she closed her eyes and let her body truly relax for the first time in the last few days. She just wanted to sleep and forget all her problems for a few hours.

30

Noah paced back and forth, from one end of his open floor plan to the other. He couldn't believe what was happening. Emma was pregnant! He was thrilled to learn he was going to become a father. Maybe now he would finally have a shot at making them a real couple. It was something he had been hoping for a long time, and he never thought he'd have the opportunity to have a life with her. But that also brought other issues to the surface.

After Emma woke up from her nap, she said she felt a lot better and wanted to go back to work. Noah didn't think it was a good idea, but he kept his mouth shut. The last thing he wanted to do was break his promise not to tell her what to do. He didn't think it was a good idea for her to go back to work so soon.

He'd admit that being in her workshop or near the ovens wouldn't hurt her or the baby, even if he would rather she stayed away from them. She had a habit of hurting herself on them, after all. And while the fumes were dangerous, Noah was aware her workshop was well ventilated so she wouldn't have a problem with breathing anything dangerous in and harming herself or the baby.

But that wasn't the only thing that was bothering him. Noah was frustrated that Emma wanted to keep yet another secret about them from everyone. Though he understood and agreed with why she wanted to keep her pregnancy a secret for the moment.

It was common for couples to keep a pregnancy to themselves for the first few months. Miscarriages often occurred in the first trimester. The last thing most women wanted to do was celebrate a new life with friends and family, then find out she lost the baby, needing to tell everyone of the loss during her time of grief.

But he didn't know how much longer he'd be able to wait to claim her publicly with their families. He felt so guilty every time he met up with Luke and Sean.

Oh, fuck! If he thought Sean was going to kill him for sleeping with his sister, he was absolutely going to kill him twice over—or torture him for days first—for getting her pregnant.

He would have to make him see that he loved Emma and wanted her to be in his life forever. She was it for him, and now they were having a baby. Of course, he couldn't tell anyone yet...because she wanted to keep them and her pregnancy a secret.

Damn it! When did his life get so complicated? He stopped in the middle of the room, his hand mussing up his hair as he ran it through. Noah had so much going on in his life, maybe it was a good idea not to tell anyone about the baby yet.

He still had the sale of the clinic being worked out. His time at the hospital was becoming more frequent—which was where he needed to be in another couple of hours and why he had the day off from the clinic today. His patients at the clinic were increasing. That only meant he was right in thinking he would need to hire more doctors and nurses sooner rather than later.

Things had calmed down with the one nurse, Marcy, thank goodness. He didn't want to keep worrying about what she would do or say next. Noah would regrettably need to let her go once he took over the clinic. He couldn't have a nurse on staff who caused problems with the other nurses, patients, or the doctors.

He couldn't do anything about it right now because, for some reason, Sid just didn't see it. But when he took over the clinic, he would take care of it. Add in juggling it all with trying to carve out time to have a relationship with Emma, who was now pregnant!

He slumped down onto the couch. He was so overwhelmed with it all. His control was always his greatest strength, and yet he was finding his life so out of control that he didn't know what to do next.

Maybe he would take a page out of Emma's book. He'd take each day at a time. Go with the flow of it all and see where it takes him. But if he did that, Noah was sure it would cause everything to fall apart. It just wasn't in his nature not to be in control of everything around him. His life had to be precise and in order.

He snorted at that. His life was now so far away from being precise and in order. Throw a baby into the mix and his life of order was about to become a case of disorder.

And somehow he couldn't be happier at the thought of his ordered apartment becoming one full of toys and other baby stuff littered all over it. He'd need to clean out that spare room to create a nursery, he thought suddenly. Crap, it was filled with...well, crap...that he just threw into the room. With his schedule, it would probably take him the whole pregnancy to clean it out and turn the room into something even partially looking like a nursery room.

Of course, once they are able to tell all their friends and family, they'll have a lot of hands to help out. His mother would love to get her hands on that room. Especially to turn it into a nursery for her first grandchild. Noah couldn't let them go through the junk he stuffed in it. He'd need to make some time to clean it out first.

No time like the present, he thought. Noah dragged himself off the couch and headed to the spare room. He had another hour before he had to get ready to go to the hospital. He'd surely make a small dent in the junk room.

31

Emma left Noah's apartment, telling him she had to go to work, but she couldn't quite bring herself to go back home or to work this morning. She needed to talk to her parents.

Luis and Erica Cooper had lunch together every afternoon. Her parents worked from home in their own offices, so they liked to 'meet' for lunch in their kitchen to reconnect.

Driving to her childhood home, she thought about all the fun she had growing up. They didn't have a large yard, but they had enough grass in the back to make it comfortable to play when it wasn't scorching hot outside. Of course, if it was really hot, their parents would set up the sprinkler to let her and Sean run through it to cool off. When they were done, they would sit on the back patio to dry off and eat popsicles.

After pulling into their driveway, she walked to the door and let herself into her parents' house. Both she and Sean each had a key to the house. Their parents always said this was as much their children's home as it was their own and so they should be able to come and go as they pleased. She wasn't always sure that was a good thing, but it was nice not to feel like a stranger in the home she grew up in.

Closing the door, she called out, "Mom, Dad, it's Emma."

"We're in the kitchen," Emma's father replied.

Her parents owned a classic colonial-style home, where all the rooms were sectioned off rather than a home with an open floor plan. The living and dining rooms were on either side of the home as she walked in. While the dining room had an open casing into the room, the living room had a smaller opening with French doors.

The stairs that led to the second floor took up a good portion of the central hallway and had a multitude of storage underneath it. At the back of the house was the kitchen, which also had a pocket door into the dining room for easy access. At the end of the hallway, a glass-framed door led to a back porch and the backyard. And to the right was a small mudroom, half bath, and laundry room.

Upstairs held all the bedrooms. One side of the home had the master bedroom suite, with a large bedroom, closet, and master bath. The other side of the home were equal-sized bedrooms with a Jack and Jill bathroom in between. This was where she and Sean had begun their plight of sharing. How they lived together now after all the chaos of growing up right next to him was a mystery to her. Though that may be why their rooms were on opposite sides of the house and they had their own bathrooms.

Their rooms didn't look like they did when they were growing up any more though. Once they both moved out, their parents turned the rooms into their own office spaces, moving their workspace out of a leased building and into their own home. Her parents did some sort of consulting work that she didn't understand, but it worked for them.

She walked down the hallway to the kitchen at the back of the house, where she found her mother sitting at the island counter and her father on the other side preparing their lunch.

"This is a nice surprise. You don't often visit in the middle of the week," her mother exclaimed.

It was out of the ordinary for her or Sean to come by during the week. Everyone was busy working—well, Emma and Sean did tend to work weird hours not really tied to specific workdays—but her parents worked Monday through Friday, so they often didn't come by to visit except on weekends.

"I had some time and figured I would join you for lunch, if that's all right," she said.

Mr. and Mrs. Cooper gave each other a confused look over the kitchen island. "We would love for you to join us," her mother said.

"Sean mentioned you weren't feeling well for the last couple of days. It doesn't look like it was anything serious," her father said.

"No. I just got some sort of stomach bug or something after spending some time with the girls, but I'm feeling better now." She didn't feel right lying to them, but she wasn't ready to tell them the truth yet. They were about to become grandparents. She was sure they would be happy for her and Noah. They would be ecstatic about becoming grandparents. But they didn't have a clue she was in a relationship with Noah, and she wasn't ready for it all to be public just yet. She had to come to terms with the fact that she was pregnant first.

"Oh, are the other girls all right?" her mother asked. "Do they need anything?"

"No one else seems to be sick, so maybe it was something only I ate. Or it didn't sit right in my stomach. Anyway...I'm fine now and ready to go back to work," she said.

No one mentioned that if she was so ready to go back to work, why was it she stopped by for lunch instead. Her parents knew it was rare for her to miss a day in her workshop. They had turned a section of their garage into one for her when she was a teenager, and she had been working almost every second she had available.

For her to be skipping prime time to work, there had to be something else going on. But her parents seemed to have an unspoken understanding that Emma was not ready to talk about it at the moment.

"Well, we're glad you are feeling better. As you can see, we're having your father's famous sandwiches for lunch. It won't take much to make another. Right, Luis?" her mother said with a smirk aimed at her husband.

He nodded with a smile of his own and took out another plate. They all teased her father about his famous sandwiches because it was about the only thing he made. They weren't anything special like the sandwiches Katia made at The Lunch Counter, but he built any type of sandwich they threw at him with no problems.

It was her parents go to for lunches now that they worked from home and since her mother made dinner for them. Growing up, everyone was always on their own for breakfast, and her parents kept it up after Emma and her brother left.

Emma slowly ate lunch with them, becoming more restless as lunch went on because she didn't want to talk to them about what was really going on and, apparently, her stomach was still a bit wobbly yet. The last thing she wanted to do was get sick at their house. They would baby her more than her brother had been, thinking she couldn't take care of herself, and may even try to encourage her to go to the doctor.

Nope...not going to happen.

So she sat at the island counter with her parents and nibbled on the sandwich—that was actually quite good—and spoke to her parents. They talked about her parent's work, Emma's work, if she was seeing anyone (Emma said no, but she knew her parents noticed her blushing by the looks they gave each other), Sean and who he was dating this time, and the

Kerrigan's (and of course she blushed again when her parents mentioned something about Noah).

Once lunch was over, Emma helped clean up the kitchen before leaving so her parents could go back to work.

She was ready to go home. Emma had to rest and think. She figured she had opened a can of worms by coming over to her parents' house. They caught everything. Emma was sure that after they talked about it between themselves, they'd have questions she wasn't ready to answer. Her parents were aware that things were not as she said they were and that she was downplaying or sidestepping everything.

Arriving home, she was glad to see that Sean was still out for the day. He had been gone a lot more since she was 'sick'... mostly because he didn't want to get sick himself. But he also had some work to do on site at the gallery for a new show that was coming up. She was intensely proud of how successful he was becoming with his paintings. He wasn't famous or anything, but he was finally getting some traction in the painting world, culminating in more galleries wanting to showcase his work.

Since he wasn't home, she removed the note she had left for him in the kitchen. No need for him to know she even went out. Though Emma was sure her parents would eventually mention seeing her. She'd deal with that when the time came.

Looking in the fridge, she was thankful to find some of the food Sean left for her, even if she was too full from lunch to eat it now. It would be perfect for dinner later on tonight. She poured herself a glass of lemon-lime soda to bring into her room with her. The light soda helped settle the remnants of unease in her stomach.

Once in her room, she closed and locked the door before opening the bag with some of the items Noah had for her at his house to help with her morning sickness. She emptied the bag out onto her night table, ensuring she had the crackers and ginger tablets ready to go. The prenatal vitamins were placed in the drawer of her nightstand. No need for Sean to accidentally see them.

She had a small mini-fridge set under the table, where she kept bottles of water and now a few bottles of the ginger ale Noah bought her. No need for her to crawl out of bed each morning until her stomach was fully settled. She didn't want to spend the mornings throwing up if she could stop it.

Sitting down on the side of her bed, she put her hand on her stomach. She was pregnant. Emma couldn't believe it, and yet it made so much sense to her now. Even with all the problems going on around her, she already loved her child more than anything. Now she just needed to figure out what to do about Noah.

32

That evening after getting home from the hospital, Noah decided he could not wait to see how Emma was doing. He had been thinking about her and the baby the entire time he was on shift. His whole concentration was shot to hell, and he almost discharged the wrong person. That would not have gone over well with his supervisor at the hospital, especially since the person he almost discharged was currently in traction...going home for him was not an option.

Thankfully, he got his head out of the clouds and realized his almost mistake before anyone else did. He got Mr. Ferguson discharged correctly, with only a little hassle when the older man was upset that it took so long to get him out of there. He was able to talk his way out of it by saying he was with another patient, which he was—it was just the wrong one.

Though he did get waylaid by a patient emergency in between, which was most likely what saved him from making the big mistake of discharging the wrong patient.

Now that he was home, he needed to know how she was feeling and make sure she was taking care of herself. Not because he thought she wasn't capable. Only that she was carrying his child and, as a doctor and a future father, he felt he had to take care of others. It wasn't just a job to him. It was who he was as a person.

It was beginning to sink in. He was going to be a father! And the person he loved almost his entire adult life was the mother. And the only thing standing in his way of having everything he ever wanted—Emma and a family of his own with her—was Emma herself. Oh, and once that hurdle was cleared, he'd add in Emma's brother to the mix. Somehow he wasn't sure that it was all going to get cleared up so cut and dried as that. Emma thought she could keep everything a secret, but they lived in a small town.

His family was huge and everywhere. And almost everyone knew everything that was going on. By this point in time, someone had noticed her parking behind his building so many times each week.

His twin, Luke, knew something was going on between them, even though Noah hadn't told him anything yet. And there was only so much time before Emma began showing her pregnancy. Their families were not stupid at all...he was honestly surprised his parents hadn't said something to him yet. When they did, he wouldn't lie to them, though he had been redirecting Luke lately.

His brother was getting more and more suspicious every time he saw him. Not about the pregnancy, obviously, since he and Emma had just found out about it that morning, but rather about them seeing each other.

Not being able to wait any longer, Noah called Emma.

"Hi, Noah," she answered.

"Hey, sweetheart. How are you feeling?" he asked. His body immediately relaxed at hearing her voice.

"I'm doing well. Just a little tired," she said.

"You're going to feel tired a lot in the first trimester. The best thing you can do is rest whenever you feel like you need to, okay?"

"I can't always lie around in bed every time I feel tired, Noah. I haven't been to my workshop in days. I have projects that need to be completed for the store and other orders," she replied in a slightly panicked tone.

He could tell she was trying to hold it all together, but she had to understand that things would have to change as her body changed during her pregnancy. He didn't want to tell her to stop working because that would just piss her off. The best option may be to let her figure it all out on her own. Right now, she wouldn't have much energy to work a lot.

As her pregnancy progressed, her back would most likely begin to hurt when she had to bend over her pottery wheel all day, or when she was lifting up some of her pottery to and from each shelf as it moved from stage to stage.

Noah was the most worried about when she was in her last trimester and was using the ovens in her workshop. Not only because she frequently burned herself but also because she had to bend over to put the pottery pieces in and out of it.

In the last few months of her pregnancy, her center of gravity would change, and she would be more susceptible to falls, or her stomach could get in the way of her being able to work in a safe way.

If he told her all of that now, she'd revolt and would no longer listen to anything he had to say. Better to go along with everything and let her figure some of it out on her own. She was still capable of working safely at this stage of her pregnancy. Once their relationship solidified further, he could bring up the possibility of needing to slow down with her work for a while.

"Of course, you can continue your work, Emma. I'm just saying you may find times when you are feeling too tired to do anything, and it's all right if you want to lie down for a rest every once in a while," he appeased her.

"Oh. Okay. I know you're right. It's just taking me a bit to realize this is all real, you know?" she asked.

He knew exactly what she was talking about. Was it really only this morning they found out she was pregnant? It felt like it was days rather than hours.

"Yes, I know what you mean. But I'm going to say one more thing at the risk of getting you upset with me again. It has to be said. Even though I'm a doctor, I'm not an OB-GYN. Luckily, there are none here in town, so you'll need to go see one at the hospital. There are several whom I trust. And if you trust me, I can get you on their schedule at a time when I'm there so we can both go together," he told her.

"Fine," she said with a sigh.

He knew she wasn't happy about it, but it was important she had the best care possible for her and the baby. It wasn't like he would be able to deliver his own baby at the hospital. He could if he had to, but it wasn't ideal.

"Thank you for not fighting me on it. I know it's not what you want, but it's important for you and the baby. I'll let you know when the appointment is." At her acceptance, he changed the subject, asking her what she did for the day.

"I stopped by my parents' house for lunch, then came home to rest. I don't want it to go to your head, but you're right. I was too tired and still a little nauseous after lunch to go into the workshop. So I came home and took a nap. I feel like all I do is sleep," she said.

"It won't be forever. And besides, once the baby is born, neither one of us will be getting much sleep at all," he said. It was the first time he had alluded to them living together after the baby was born.

"I'm not even ready to start thinking about not sleeping after the baby is born. I'm still coming to terms with the fact that I'm pregnant at all. My brain still wants to believe it's just the stomach flu," she replied.

He supposed she was still too tired to have caught him telling her they would be living together once the baby was born. It was a risk to mention it so soon. She still wasn't ready to tell everyone about them, never mind about the pregnancy. Which made him think. How could she have hidden it from her parents? They were pretty astute. Did they ask her why she wasn't feeling well, then put the pieces together themselves?

"So I was wondering. Did you tell your parents about me and the baby?" Another risk, but he couldn't seem to help himself from asking. He knew he was going to piss her off, but he was getting frustrated that she wouldn't be in a relationship with him publicly. And now they were going to have a baby!

"I already said I'm not ready to tell anyone about our relationship or the baby. Geeez! We just found out I'm pregnant...give me some time to let it sink in. Please!" she begged. "Besides, I'm not sure I want anyone to know at all. Imagine all the chaos that will happen if our families find out. Maybe it would be best if I didn't tell them ever."

Noah was ready to let it go when she pleaded with him to give her some time, but then she went and said she might not want to tell anyone about them. That meant no one would know he was the father of her baby.

Did she think he would let her raise their baby on her own? Never see his own child or have to sneak around to visit.

Hell no! That was not going to happen.

She didn't know it yet, but they were going to get married, she was going to move into his apartment, they were going to fix up the second bedroom and turn it into a nursery, then they were going to have the baby and raise him or her together. In that order even!

"So what if our families found out? We're adults, Emma. They really don't have a say in our lives. Besides, our families will not only be fine with it, but the real concern right now should be for our baby, not how others will react," he said. Their parents would be ecstatic knowing they were together and having a baby. As for her brother, well, once Sean calms down and gets used to it, he'd be fine, too.

"Exactly! We need to think about what is best for the baby right now, and that means I need to keep everything to ourselves. It hasn't even been a day, Noah."

He could hear how exhausted she was through the phone. It wouldn't do any good to batter at her over and over about telling their families right now. Besides, she was right. It was too soon to tell anyone about the baby. She was only about six weeks pregnant, but they couldn't keep it a secret forever. When he said as much to her, she agreed, stating that it was obvious her pregnancy couldn't be kept a secret forever, but as for the rest, she needed time.

Noah told her to get some sleep and that he would talk to her tomorrow. After hanging up, he pondered why Emma wanted to keep them a secret so badly. Yes, he understood how her brother might react. He was his best friend after his own brother after all.

But her parents would be thrilled. His family always got along with her family. And Mr. and Mrs. Cooper would also be thrilled with a grandchild. So would his parents.

He decided to give her some more time to get through her first trimester before he pressured her again to tell everyone. No need to get her all worked up before she even saw the OB-GYN and found out if everything with the baby was okay. He was getting ahead of himself for sure. But he couldn't help it. It wasn't every day that he found out he was going to be a father.

33

Over the next couple of weeks, Emma's morning sickness was diminishing as she continued working in her workshop. And tried to avoid Noah. Not that it worked. She couldn't totally ignore him no matter how hard she told herself to.

He would stop by her workshop to bring her healthy food and more prenatal vitamins when she ran out. She realized he was frustrated with her for not wanting to tell everyone about them and the baby, but he had also been good at making sure she was taken care of without having to go to the clinic or drugstore.

The wonders of small-town life. Emma wouldn't be able to avoid it forever. She just needed this time to come to grips with it all.

And she was getting there. The couple of trips she made to the hospital for appointments Noah set up for her with the OB-GYN helped her out a lot. Not just with the realization that she was pregnant, but that he was supportive of her and the baby.

He chose the perfect doctor for her. Dr. Giselle Brown was kind and discreet, as were the staff in her office. Usually, she would have only been seen the one time at this stage, but Noah convinced the doctor to set up another appointment for them to do an ultrasound. He said he wanted to make sure they were starting out the pregnancy with no issues.

Dr. Brown said she would humor him, knowing how hard it was not to think about everything that could go wrong as a doctor. So they went in another time for an ultrasound and a few more tests. Everything looked good, by the way, but it did make being pregnant feel more real.

Today, Emma needed to go downtown to drop off a lot of her projects that had been piling up. The morning sickness was still making itself known, but it was better—or rather, she now knew not to rush out of bed in the mornings before nibbling on a ginger tablet and sipping some water. Her energy was starting to come back, too.

She was nearing the second trimester, and that meant it was approaching the time she needed to make a decision on how to tell the people in her life she was pregnant. And whether that included telling them about Noah. She wasn't nearly ready to think about any of it yet.

Instead, she concentrated on work. So much time was spent away from her workshop that projects piled up, while others were sitting incomplete; the shops she did business with were running out of stock. Her first priority was to package up everything she had completed in the workshop and deliver it to the main shop she did business with. The others had more specific requirements, and those were still in the process of being completed. She'd get to those tomorrow.

Emma carefully packaged all of her creations for the trip into crates, then tried to fit them all into her ridiculously small vehicle. Every space was filling up, yet she had only placed a couple of crates inside. Stupid car. Why did she buy such a small car in the first place? Oh yeah. The whole *'hey my last name is Cooper and here's a cute Mini Cooper....hahaha'* thing. Right now? Nope, not that funny anymore.

Besides, she thought as she looked at the car, she couldn't imagine what it would be like getting in and out of the small car once she was as big as a house. She'd be bigger than the car.

Okay...nope, she didn't want to think about that yet either.

But seriously, it was going to be hard once the baby was born to fit a baby carrier in and out of the car. Plus all the stuff a baby needed each day. Where would she put it all?

The car was a two-door with a hardtop. She couldn't even put the roof down to put the baby carrier into the backseat. This was another thing she would need to think about. She couldn't afford a new car. This one was dying a slow death, but it worked well enough for her. Her plan when she bought it was to run it until it didn't run anymore.

But she didn't consider how her life would change so quickly. Hadn't considered she would need room for transporting her pottery or a baby.

Granted, she didn't often need to use it for transporting the bulk of her work. Usually, she would bring in a couple of pieces at a time, and when she had larger shipments, Sean helped her move everything from her workshop to the shops with his larger SUV. He was busy this morning doing who knew what, and she couldn't wait for him to become available.

As she was moving a packing crate to her car, Noah pulled up to the workshop in a Jeep with a trailer attached. Of course he would show up now. He was probably going to tell her she couldn't do this by herself. That it was too dangerous for her to carry the crates or some crap like that.

Noah hopped out of the Jeep, opened the trailer doors, before walking over to her to take the crate out of her hands.

"Good morning, sweetheart," he said, giving her a quick kiss on the lips.

"What are you doing here?" she asked him. She was

suspicious of his reasons for showing up. And how the hell did he know she was moving crates today, anyway?

"Sean mentioned that you had a lot of inventory to bring over to the shop downtown, but he couldn't make it to help you. Since today happens to be my day off, I volunteered to come by and help out. I stopped by Oliver and Demi's house and asked to borrow her Jeep and trailer. And so here I am," he said.

"That's it?" she asked suspiciously.

"Of course, why else would I be here? No, wait, there is something else. I get to spend the day with you," he said with a smile.

He looked like a kid who knew he had just gotten away with something. Noah was rarely anything but serious. So, seeing him looking so relaxed and smiling, had her relaxed and smiling, too. He left her standing in place, while he deposited the crate into the trailer.

"No lecture?" she asked when he walked back over to her.

"You have been doing this by yourself forever, and you're perfectly capable of still moving the crates. Of course, as you progress through your pregnancy, it will be harder to do because your center of gravity will be off. For today it's okay," he said, hesitating for a moment. "But if you want to leave the heavier, more awkwardly shaped items for me to move, I won't be opposed to taking care of them for you."

She was amazed at the lack of lecture and his ability to let things go that concerned him. He had been worried about her every time they were together. So this was a nice change of pace.

"Okay then. I could use some help. The Jeep and trailer will also be useful. Apparently my Mini Cooper isn't up for the task of transporting everything I need to bring today," she said.

"Well, let's start with moving everything out of that Mini Cooper and into the trailer," he said, before pulling her into a hug. "And if it's okay, we can check out the mini Cooper—no wait...the mini Kerrigan—growing inside you with another ultrasound later this afternoon."

He eased away from her and began unloading her car into the trailer, while she stood with her mouth gaping open. Noah was a sneaky one, she thought. She knew he couldn't stop worrying for long. And somehow she didn't mind that one bit.

34

Once in town, Noah parked the Jeep and trailer behind the shops in the area for deliveries. They got out of the car and walked around to the front of the building to let the shop owner, Sharlene, know they had arrived and to open the door in back for them.

The bell jingled above the door as it opened. As the door closed, a woman approached them from the back of the store.

"Mom. I didn't realize you were working this morning," he said.

"Oh, I wasn't supposed to, but I thought I'd drop in to help Sharlene. She told me yesterday Emma was coming by with a large delivery. I didn't expect to see you, too," his mother, Amanda Kerrigan, said with a twinkle in her eyes, as she leaned in for a hug.

"Sean said he wouldn't be able to help Emma, so I volunteered since it's my day off," he replied.

"Hi, Emma. It's so nice to see you again," his mother said, also leaning in to give her a hug. His mother was a hugger, and he was all right with that.

"Hi, Mrs. Kerrigan," she said. "Thanks for being here to help with the delivery. I know Sharlene wouldn't say so, but it's probably too much for her to unpack all on her own."

Artisan Crafts and Art was a wonderful store that held all manner of art, specifically from local artists but also from any who lived in the area all the way down to Orlando.

Sharlene Walton opened her store after the death of her second husband five years ago. She always said that she had lost the love of her life when she was barely eighteen. Not to death, but to a lack of maturity and life experiences. But then she met someone else ten years later and married again, living a good and happy life she was proud of. The store was a celebration of that life and the one she hoped for with her first husband.

She wasn't what Noah would consider old—she was in her 60s and looked like she was in her late 40s, if that—but after loading all the crates into the trailer, he'd have to agree the woman shouldn't have to unpack all of them herself.

Some of the pieces were rather heavy or had odd shapes to them, which made it difficult to maneuver. Thinking about it, he should offer to help her later to unpack those pieces, or find someone else who had more time to help.

"How many times do I need to tell you to call me Amanda?" his mother said affectionately. "Now, let's go find Sharlene and get you unloaded. I'm sure you both have other things to do."

The look she gave him made him wary. She was up to something, but he couldn't guess what it was. With his mother, it could be anything.

Noah was ready to unload the trailer. He may have the day off, but he did schedule an ultrasound for later that afternoon for Emma.

They headed toward the back of the shop and found the store owner doing some paperwork in the office.

"Sharlene, Emma and Noah are here with her wonderful pottery pieces," Amanda said.

"Oh good! Emma darling, we are almost out of your stock. And I can't wait to check out the other pieces you told me you created," she said.

The woman was like a flower child of the 70s. She was decked out in a long flowy skirt, colorful blouse, and enough bangles on each arm that she jingled every time she made a movement. On her feet, she wore ballerina flats—at least that's what the triplets told him they were called—so she barely reached the middle of his chest.

Sharlene was a little hippy, a little southern, and the nicest woman you'd ever meet. She was also a busy-body, nosy woman who had to have her pulse on everything around her and make sure everyone else knew what was going on as well. Her personality was one contradiction after another.

"Where is Sean this morning? I see you have a different helper today," Sharlene said.

Here they went again. Maybe they should put out a sign: *"Sean is busy, so I volunteered to help."*

Not that he expected it to help or anything. The woman wanted any gossip available. And because she was so nice, with that southern drawl that made those around her feel like they were sitting on a porch drinking sweet tea, everyone had to be careful not to spill any information they didn't want spread all over the town by dinner.

Noah half-listened to Emma talking to the shop owner and his mother. Would it really be all that bad if something slipped and the whole town found out about them? It may be a problem for Emma, but it would solve his need to tell everyone they were together and having a baby. She couldn't blame him if the shop owner started blabbing her mouth about what she suspected about them. But he wouldn't do that to her. He loved her enough to understand he couldn't push her beyond what she was ready for...at least for now.

As this was running through his head, they began unloading the trailer one crate at a time. He enlisted his mother to help him with the larger pieces, knowing that both of them carrying them would lighten the load and keep Emma from trying to lift them herself.

He didn't realize that he often touched her as they passed each other, looked at her with love and affection in his eyes, or that his mother caught the exchanges.

Nor did he know that his mother thought Emma's mother was right. When Erica Cooper contacted Amanda after her daughter's visit she told her something was going on with them, and there was the possibility Emma was pregnant with their first grandchild. They made plans to discuss it further once Amanda Kerrigan got her eyes on the pair to confirm for herself. .

When everything was unloaded, Noah stood outside with Emma while his mother and Sharlene went back inside to work.

"Mom said we can leave the Jeep and trailer parked here while we go to lunch," he told her.

She sighed. "I need to go back to the workshop. I'm too far behind to stick around, so if you could just drop me off, I'd appreciate it."

"Not going to happen. You need to eat, and no one will find out anything about us just because we have lunch together. After we eat, I'll take you back to your workshop for an hour while I drop off the Jeep and trailer at Demi and Oliver's place. Then I'll pick you up for the ultrasound appointment at the hospital," he told her.

She wasn't happy about his steamrolling over her, but he wasn't budging on any of it. He saw when she realized this, too, her shoulders slumping a little with defeat, though her eyes narrowed and she gave him her most aggrieved stare.

He liked that she didn't back down even when she didn't like him steamrolling her into doing what he wanted her to—at least when it came to her health and that of their baby.

With that resolved, they walked around the building to the sidewalk downtown and headed toward Katia's deli sandwich shop.

35

They walked in silence. But inside her head, Emma was seething and yet not. She didn't like that Noah kept on telling her what to do, but she also liked how he took care of her. He made sure she ate and seemed to know exactly what she needed, even if she didn't want to tell him he was right. She had to maintain some control over the situation.

Of course, she was happy to have had the help today. It was great of him to show up and to ask for Demi's Jeep and trailer. It made hauling all her pottery and wall art pieces easier to transport. She would have been making trips back and forth all day otherwise. She silently snorted.

This was the first time she had brought her wall art pieces in. They were part of the collection she was experimenting with, and now that she saw how they fit in the trailer, Emma wasn't sure they would have even fit in her car. She would have had to strap them onto the roof, and she didn't think they would make it from her workshop to the downtown shop in one piece.

So she would go to lunch with him, take her measly hour to

work, then go with him to the hospital for yet another ultrasound, which she knew was for his own benefit rather than something Dr. Brown ordered.

She wouldn't tell him she had no plans to work for the hour he left her at the workshop. Her body still drained of energy on occasion, and all the work of moving the pieces from the workshop to the trailer and then from the trailer into the shop was enough to wear her out.

When they arrived at Katia's sandwich and deli shop, The Lunch Counter, Noah opened the door for her and they both walked in.

Katia's place was located at the corner of the long line of shops and restaurants. With its large windows on two sides, it was bright and airy. Under those windows sat long countertops with high-backed stools in black metal and dark mahogany seats. Patrons were already sitting, some with laptops out, some with earbuds in, and all with one of Katia's prime sandwiches in front of them.

Along the back wall was the deli, a glass case showcasing the selections, where locals often came to stock up on fresh lunch meats and cheeses. Already a small line formed to place their order, while one employee took the next guest, another was busy cutting slices off a huge chunk of meat.

On the other wall was the sandwich station. It too had a line, though not a long one yet, as they came in before the lunch rush. That would soon change since Katia only opened The Lunch Counter from eleven to three, though she often worked longer hours.

Behind the counter was a shelf full of bread, delivered fresh that morning. A fridge with glass doors showed pre-sliced meats and cheeses ready to be made into some of Katia's creations. Mahogany tables that matched the stools located at the counters, along with bright red chairs, filled the center of the restaurant.

"Noah! Emma!" Katia called out from behind the sandwich station when they walked in.

"Hey, Katia. How's my favorite cousin?" Noah said with a smirk.

"Oh, stop it. I know better than to fall for that. Try it with someone else," she said with a laugh.

"Hi Katia," Emma said.

"What brings both of you here this afternoon?" Katia asked.

"I was bringing new stock into the shop, and Noah came to help when Sean couldn't make it," she responded.

"And we couldn't pass up the opportunity to stop by for lunch. You make the best sandwiches in town," he added.

She nodded her head in agreement. It was one area they both agreed on, as did most of the locals. Noah's cousin made typical sandwiches like the BLT, Reuben, and a killer cheesesteak sub. But she also experimented with new creations and sandwiches that would be found in more expensive sandwich shops or restaurants.

They had a turkey sandwich on focaccia with thick slices of mozzarella melted onto the bread, pesto and tomatoes that was one of her favorites. Her mouth was already watering just thinking about it. They both ordered, making small talk with Katia as she made their sandwiches.

"Do you or your parents know of any places available to rent?" she asked Noah.

"Are you looking for herself?" Noah asked.

"No, it's for Marinda. She needs a place in a couple of months. Her apartment complex is doing renovations, and she needs to move soon. Marinda's not telling us much more about it though, and I'm not sure why. I haven't gotten it out of her yet, but I will," she said with a glint in her eye.

The triplets were relentless when they wanted information, even from each other. It seemed there were no secrets allowed among the three of them—or so Ryleigh told her at one time.

"Why doesn't she just move in with you?" he said with a shrug. Katia and Emma looked at each other and rolled their eyes.

Emma told him, "They may be sisters, but that doesn't mean they want to live with each other."

"You live with your brother," he pointed out.

"I wouldn't even do that if I could afford not to live with someone. Besides, my brother was a better bet than living with a roommate I didn't really know."

Noah shrugged as though it were no big deal to him. And yet he lived by himself rather than with his own brother or one of his friends. "I don't know of any places, but I'll let Marinda know if I hear anything. I can ask my parents, too."

Emma and Katia shared another look and a smile before she handed them their sandwiches. Noah paid for their meal and drinks, then picked up the tray. They turned to find a table and were startled to discover Marcy right behind them.

"Noah," she said. "What a surprise."

"Marcy. You remember Emma," he said, still holding the tray in front of him.

Emma was slightly surprised to hear him speak to his nurse so harshly. She thought they worked well together, and she was the only one who was uncomfortable around the woman.

Marcy looked at her as if she had something rotten all over her before responding, "Oh sure. Sean's sister, right?"

"Enjoy your day off," he said and somehow got her moving toward a table.

They sat down, and he divvied up the food and drinks between them, moving the tray off to the side.

"I don't trust her," Noah spat out softly, still looking over to where his nurse was now at the counter ordering her lunch from one of the other employees.

"You don't? I thought I was the only one," she said, surprised at his words.

"Nope. And I'm still not sure why Sean is still seeing her either."

He didn't go into more of his reasons while they began eating and instead changed the subject to ask questions about some of the pottery and wall art they had just delivered.

Once done with their meal, he scooped up the trash and threw it all away.

"Come on, let's get you back to the workshop so I can drop off the Jeep and trailer. We don't want to be late for your appointment," he said.

Resigned that she wasn't going to have her own way, she let him lead her toward the door of The Lunch Counter. Secretly, she liked his taking charge of what she needed to do with the pregnancy, but she wouldn't tell him that just yet.

───

Marcy grabbed her lunch from the counter then sauntered over to a table to eat, glaring at the couple a few tables away. She knew Noah was looking at her after he sat down, but now he was faced away from her and not paying her any attention.

She couldn't let that go. She was aware of how he felt about her, and sitting with the disheveled girl to make her jealous wasn't going to work.

When she saw they were ready to leave, Marcy quickly wrapped up the rest of her sandwich. Stepping up behind them on her way toward the door, she ran her hand across Noah's lower back as she came around him. She was thrilled with how he jumped at the contact.

"It was nice seeing you both, and I'll see you at work tomorrow," she told Noah, giving him a suggestive look. "And maybe I'll see you again soon at the clinic," she told Emma.

The girl looked confused, wondering what she was talking about. Good! She was glad she was uncomfortable with her.

Maybe the more time she spent around Noah and Sean, the more uncomfortable she'd become and move on. The girl was a threat to her being able to have Noah all to herself.

As she was about to leave, Marcy couldn't resist another dig. "You let Sean know I had a wonderful time and I'm waiting for his call."

Not giving either of them time to respond, she walked out of the building, down the sidewalk and to her parked car located near the shop they all started from. As she walked, she thought about the juicy info she had learned. Marcy would use it to break up Emma and Noah.

When she first entered the store, no one was around, so she just took her time browsing. Then she heard people talking in the back, going in and out of the back door.

Recognizing Noah's voice, she left the store and went around to the back. Peeking around the corner, she spotted him go into a small trailer, then come out with a crate. Others were with him doing the same. His mother, the store owner, and Emma.

Why would he be helping her out? That made no sense to Marcy. She was just a girl, playing at being a woman. Most of the time, all she wore were jeans and ratty t-shirts covered with clay. The girl did clean up well the one time she saw her at that party. Hence the playing at being a woman.

When all four were inside the store, she hurried to her car and crouched down behind it, watching how Noah—her Noah—gave the girl light touches or heated looks as they passed each other.

No! He was hers!

When they had finished loading everything in and said goodbye to the other two, she expected them to leave. Instead of getting into the Jeep and driving away though, they stood for a moment talking.

She overheard them talk about being a couple and going to the hospital for an ultrasound. Marcy had added those details to the day she witnessed Noah leave the clinic with prenatal vitamins.

Following them to The Lunch Counter was just her way to

get inside their heads. And she would admit the food was delicious.

But now she almost had all she needed. Getting into her car, she drove away, planning what she'd do with the new information.

36

A couple of days later, Noah was working at the clinic, stewing about Emma wanting to keep their relationship and her pregnancy from their families. But it was getting to him every time he was around his brother, parents, and Sean. Luke was his twin, and not telling him was wearing on him. They told each other everything... always had and always will.

Though Luke had been a bit more secretive in the last few years. Ever since he got hurt the first time while serving overseas in the military, he clammed up. It wasn't a serious injury, so once he healed, he went right back to work with his unit. Then something happened. He was hurt again, and he refused to talk about why he got out and came home.

That really bothered Noah. Something wasn't right, and the secrets were getting to him. Luke had been hiding whatever was bothering him, and he couldn't help him if he didn't know what it was. But that was for another time. He would figure out what was going on with his brother once he got his own shit together with Emma.

Noah couldn't take it anymore. With some time between patients, he slipped into his office to make a quick call to

Emma. As the phone rang, he wondered what he was doing. Was he really going to risk upsetting her? Yes, he had to. He couldn't let his feelings about all the secrecy go on any longer. She was carrying his child. And he wanted to tell everyone about it. Why should they keep it from their families? It wasn't like it would remain a secret for much longer, anyway.

"Hey, Noah. What's up? You don't usually call me when you're working," she said, concern in her voice filtering through.

He knew calling her during his work day would worry her. Clinic hours meant he spent his day moving from one room to another, visiting with his patients. Noah only took a few moments in between to type up his notes before moving on to the next patient. Sometimes he didn't even have the opportunity to grab lunch, though he'd been sneaking out now and then to find a way to deliver a healthy lunch to Emma on occasion.

"I can't do it anymore," he told her.

"You can't do what anymore?" she cautiously asked.

"I need to tell my family what is going on between us and about the baby. It's not right to keep it from our families, Emma." He was risking it all, but this just couldn't go on. She was already showing a small baby bump. It was only a matter of time before someone noticed.

"There is nothing going on between us, and the baby is my concern, not yours," she responded, the little hitch in her voice giving her away.

Noah was livid. "There is absolutely something going on between us, and the baby is absolutely my concern. I won't be pushed to the side and treated as though I'm not the father."

At this, Marcy walked into his office, a look of surprise on her face. "I'm sorry for interrupting. You have a patient waiting in room two."

"I'll be right there," he said through clenched teeth, watching her walk out the door. Damn, damn, damn.

"What was that?" Emma asked, with slight panic in her voice.

"Nothing. I need to go, but we will be talking about this more later," he warned, hanging up before she was able to speak another word.

Shit. Now what was he going to do? He wanted Emma to agree to let him start telling his family, but then his nurse walked in at the wrong time when he was talking about being the father. Maybe she didn't hear anything. And maybe their news was about to be announced before Emma was ready for it. Damn, damn, damn.

Why did he need to call her now? He should have waited until he was back home after work to have this conversation. Then to have Marcy walk in! Any other employee of the clinic and he wouldn't be concerned. Marcy, though, had already been proven untrustworthy.

What were they going to do if she did overhear his conversation about Emma being pregnant with his child? Not much, he admitted.

Maybe what he wanted all along—to tell their families about their relationship and the baby—would now occur. So if he was getting what he wanted, why was he feeling panicked over it?

It was because of Emma. She was going to go ballistic if Sean found out. Especially if he found out due to Noah's inability to wait to have that conversation.

Noah didn't have time to contemplate his actions or the repercussions of those actions. There was nothing he could do about it now, and he had a patient waiting for him. Pocketing his phone, he left his office and headed to room two.

With a quick knock, he entered the room. "Good afternoon, Mrs. Everett. What brings you in today?"

37

Emma was so angry with Noah for putting her in this position. She was not ready to tell anyone about the baby, and he should understand why. Her brother was one of his best friends. She had to live with Sean, and if he got involved in this whole thing right now, she'd never hear the end of it.

Emma wouldn't be able to keep it a secret forever, but this was her life, damn it! She was the one having the baby, not him! He was a doctor. Shouldn't he understand that Emma wanted a little more time to figure things out? She was still in her first trimester. Of course, now they knew that wasn't really true. The last ultrasound put her due date a little earlier than they first figured.

But that wasn't the point. If he couldn't be supportive of her decisions, then she couldn't be with him. He would just need to deal with it. Emma wouldn't keep the baby from him, but she couldn't be with him anymore.

And what was that at the end of their call? Did someone come in when he was talking about being the father? No, no, no. That didn't happen. No way was her news about the pregnancy about to be exposed by someone who happened to overhear his phone conversation.

Why would he put her in this position by calling at work, anyway? Nope, it was definitely over. She couldn't be with someone who didn't think about how she felt.

Decision firmly made, Emma called Noah, knowing he would be with patients and couldn't answer his phone. It may be the coward's way out, but she wasn't in the right frame of mind to care right now.

The phone rang and rang and rang until his voicemail picked up.

You have reached Noah Kerrigan. Leave a message.

Short and to the point. It was just like him not to flaunt his position. No Dr. Kerrigan or all those letters he had behind his name on his voicemail. Being a doctor was just who he was. It was his life, not a means to extract authority over others or make himself seem more important. The thought had her wavering over what she was about to do, but at the beep she became resolute that this must be done.

"Noah, this is Emma. If you can't understand why I don't want to say anything to anyone yet about us or the baby, then I don't want to see you anymore. We'll work something out once the baby is born, but until then I don't want anything to do with you. I'll keep my scheduled appointments with Dr. Brown. She can prescribe me the prenatal vitamins. And I'll give them permission to talk to you about the baby and show you any ultrasounds. But for now, that's it. Bye."

Phone call made, Emma went about getting ready to head into her workshop for the day. She was going in a little later than usual due to some lingering morning sickness, but it couldn't be put off anymore. She had a baby to support and needed to work.

On her drive to the workshop, the guilt began to fester in a tiny corner of her mind. Was she too harsh? Too impulsive? Her father was always telling her that she often leaped before thinking things through. Was this another one of those times? Granted, many of those leaps led her to pottery and to becoming the person she was today. If she thought things through too much, then she'd never have gone off to apprentice in pottery so young. Or bought the house with Sean.

Of course, there were some instances where the leap probably should have waited until she thought things through a bit first. Was this one of those times? Did she just make a big mistake breaking it off with Noah when she was about to have his baby? An ache in her chest formed at the thought of not having him in her life on a daily basis.

No! She had to stick with what she felt in this moment. She should never have been put in the position of being forced to tell others about them or the baby before she was ready.

Standing by her decision, Emma pulled up to her workshop and got out of the car. Locking it, she walked to the door, unlocking and opening the main door to the right before walking inside. She flipped the switch next to the door as it closed, illuminating the entire workspace.

The door was supposed to lock when it closed, but something was wrong with the mechanism. Emma had no idea what that meant, only that it didn't lock automatically and she had to flip the lock. It was a pain because she frequently forgot to do it.

On separate occasions, Sean and Noah had both found it unlocked and gave her hell about it. They were worried she was unsafe working alone. The place had a doorbell and security camera with a small monitor by the door her father set up. Emma glanced at it before unlocking and opening the door for anyone.

She often didn't hear the bell anyway if she was deep into her work. That was why her parents and Sean had a key to the workshop.

She gave one to Noah, too. Damn...now she would need to

get that back if they were no longer together. With that thought, she flipped the lock to secure herself inside. No need to make it any easier for him, she thought. A quick slice of guilt once again flashed through her before she brushed it off.

Nope. No time for those thoughts. She needed to concentrate on work. Walking over to the center table, she set her bag and keys down, then set about making a plan of where to start.

38

That night, Noah was going to meet Luke at The Bar downtown. He was still upset over Emma's voicemail and was struggling about whether to say anything to Luke or not. He didn't feel good about keeping secrets from his twin, and he was confused about what to do with Emma and the baby. He needed someone who knew him to talk it out. There was no one better than his own twin.

Besides, he'd been trying all afternoon since hearing Emma's message to contact her. She was definitely ignoring him. Not one peep out of her. Her phone message told him she was upset. He should let her cool off before trying to find her, but he couldn't let it go. He loved her too much to throw away what they already had, and he wouldn't let her throw him away either.

And she was carrying his baby. If she thought he would just stand by and take scraps of information about the baby's development inside her, then she was mistaken. He suspected she knew full well he wouldn't take it. Which was probably why she was ignoring him now.

He wasn't sure how much Marcy had overheard when he

185

was talking to Emma on the phone. If she heard him say anything about being the father, Emma's whole plan of trying to keep it to themselves was blown to pieces. With his nurse dating Sean, who knew what she would say to him?

Of course, Marcy never said anything to Noah when he joined her in the exam room or any time throughout the rest of the work shift. She didn't even look at him in any way that indicated she heard his side of the conversation. So, he assumed they were safe.

Walking up to The Bar, the noise from the music and people talking came through the doors, spilling out into the night. The sound blasted as he opened the door. A long bar stretched from one end of the room to the other, with three bartenders working behind it. Stools ran the length of the bar, almost every one filled to capacity. Televisions flashed — behind the bar and in each corner of the room —showing the patrons various sporting events, commercials, and the weather.

The rest of the room was filled with tables and chairs, some seating four, others seating only two, and a few high tops along the back wall next to the hallway to the restrooms. About half were already taken. It wouldn't be long before the place was packed.

Music played out of an ancient jukebox—that for some reason only played songs from the 60s, 70s and 80s—and two large speakers situated on either side of it. The wood floor was scarred, but shiny. He figured they used a bunch of polyurethane to give them that just-waxed look.

Searching around the room, he spotted his brother sitting at a table in the corner, away from the jukebox. Neither he nor Luke came to The Bar to sit and listen to music. They liked being able to talk to each other without the need to scream.

Noah looked toward the jukebox and shook his head at how many people were sitting close to it. And as expected, they were either not talking to each other, sitting extremely close together to talk practically into their ears, or yelling across their table, increasing the noise inside.

He walked to the table, pulled out a chair and sat down. "Hey, thanks for meeting me here."

Instead of replying immediately, Luke gave a quick gesture and a look to the waitress a couple of tables away, picked up his beer and took a sip. "I ordered you a beer when I got in," he said a moment later.

"Thanks. I sure could use one," Noah said, letting out a deep breath. This was the first time all week he had felt like he could breathe and relax.

Who was he kidding? It had been more than a week since he had felt that way.

The waitress weaved her way through the tables to them, a beer in one hand, some napkins in the other. When she made it to their table, she slapped a napkin down, then plopped the beer on top of it. "Here you go, Doc. Anything else I can get for either of you?" she asked.

"Not right now, Hollie," Luke told her. She nodded to them both, then sauntered off to take care of other tables.

They spent the next few minutes sitting next to each other in silence, each watching the television screens over the bar and drinking their beer. Well, Noah was not really drinking his beer. Instead, he was picking at the label on the bottle, ignoring that Luke kept on eyeing him suspiciously.

His brother set his beer down hard on the table. "Something is wrong."

He continued to ignore his twin some more. This wasn't the place to talk about everything that was bugging him, but he couldn't keep it in anymore. It wasn't like everyone wasn't going to find out sooner rather than later.

"Maybe you should just spit it out," Luke said.

Noah sighed, put down his beer, and looked at Luke. "Emma and I have been dating, and she's pregnant."

He watched as Luke opened and closed his mouth several times. His brother didn't talk a lot, not because he didn't know what to say, but because he was someone who chose his words carefully. When Luke spoke, it meant something. He was a watcher and listener, along with never being surprised about anything he had seen or heard. It was what made him a good sheriff and what probably made him a good soldier. That Luke seemed flabbergasted over what Noah just said was significant.

"I didn't see that one coming," he said. "Sean is going to kill you."

"I know." Noah gave an unamused half-chuckle before they directed their attention back to the television screens.

They finished their beers and got another from their waitress before picking up the conversation again.

"Do you have a problem with becoming a father?" Luke asked.

"No, I don't. But that's not really the problem. Emma doesn't want to tell anyone about us or the baby. And today, when I told her I felt it was best to tell everyone, Emma broke up with me over voicemail," Noah explained, letting him listen to the message.

"Ouch," his brother said, lifting his beer for another sip.

"Right? I'm not really sure what to do now. I'm not going to sit on the sidelines while she goes in for check-ups, getting scraps of information from her doctor. As if I'm consulting on a patient's case with another doctor. And she's not going to be keeping it secret forever. At some point she's not going to be able to hide the pregnancy. Sean will wonder who the father is, as will her parents. She'd need to tell them then. And they'll all think I was blowing it off and not supporting her if she continues to keep me at arm's length. Screw that!" Noah said, getting riled up again over her voicemail.

"I think you should tell Mom and Dad. They need to know

you are going to be a father, and they can support you with Emma's family if things go sideways," he said.

"I've thought about it. But I'm already feeling guilty for telling you about us and the baby. She really didn't want anyone to find out yet."

"Just tell her I figured it out. Honestly, I've been wondering what was going on with you two ever since Oliver and Demi's engagement party. Before then, really. You've had it bad for her for years, little brother," he said.

"I was born before you," Noah complained.

"I was named first," Luke countered.

It was an old argument that lightened up the conversation. It was true that Luke was named first. In the womb, he was baby A, while Noah was baby B. So they named his brother, Luke Jr. after their father, though he went by Lou. Noah was named after their mother's father, Noah Laine. But he had been in a hurry to come out, while Luke wanted to take his time— slow and steady from the start.

So Noah was born first, then Luke. And yet, his twin was always saying he was meant to be born first, only Noah was in a hurry as usual and bumped him out of the way, so technically he was the older brother. It was complete garbage.

One of the pub employees raised the volume on the television showing the weather. The latest updates on a hurricane that just formed in the Gulf of Mexico were being discussed. The meteorologists were saying it may impact the Gulf Coast of Florida and reach inland, and be just as devastating to those inland as it would be to those on the coast.

"That's the last thing I need to deal with right now," Luke complained.

His tone caught Noah's attention. "What else has been going on? Everything okay with you?"

"Yeah, everything's good, just don't want to deal with a hurricane right now," Luke muttered.

They continued to watch the forecast, each thinking about what they would need to do to prepare for such a storm. He should gather up some medical supplies and make sure they had enough in case they got called out to help people injured who couldn't make it to the hospital.

Luke interrupted his thoughts. "You need to tell Sean."

Yeah, he was aware he had to tell Sean. But would he survive it?

<h1 style="text-align:center">39</h1>

Later that night, Emma was sitting in the living room watching a TV show.

She was in the middle of ruminating over what to do when Sean came home from his date.

"Hey, how was your date?" she asked him. She was fishing a bit because he went out with Marcy again, and she wasn't sure if she liked the woman or not.

Sean grunted, and she looked up at him from the couch. He stalked over to the kitchen island, leaning his back against it facing her. He looked upset. His arms were crossed over his chest, and he was glaring off into the distance.

"Did your date not go well?" she asked.

"Oh, my date went fine, but I was told something that concerned me," he said.

Emma had an uncomfortable thought about what it was he was told but couldn't help but ask, "What did you hear that has you so upset?"

"That you're dating Noah and are pregnant. Tell me the information is wrong, Emma," he accused.

Emma gasped at his words. No, this was not happening.

Who told him about them? No one other than Noah and Dr. Brown knew about them or the baby. Unless the person who walked into Noah's office when he called her was Marcy. That bitch! Now, she absolutely didn't like that woman.

Pretending she didn't know what he was talking about, she asked, "Who did you hear that from? Sounds like someone is messing with you, Sean."

"It doesn't matter who I heard it from, is it true?" he asked.

Emma got up from the couch. She was angry that he would take the word of one of his bimbos over her own. Sure, he was right. She was dating Noah—at least until earlier today—and she was pregnant. But that was not the point. Her brother should support her, not listen to gossip from one of his many 'girlfriends'.

"What difference does it make, Sean? Obviously, you already know the truth, so why should I bother telling you anything? It wouldn't be like you'd believe me," she said, glaring back.

"What difference does it make? Seriously!" Sean's temper exploded.

"Butt out, Sean! You're not in charge of me, so stay out of it," she yelled. No one would ever accuse her of cowering when her brother got angry.

"I can't do that. Noah was my best friend, and he took advantage of you. And now I need to take care of it and him," he said.

"I'm not a little girl. I can take care of myself. I'm not some innocent, and Noah didn't take advantage of me, so leave it alone. It's none of your business!"

Sean walked up to her and wrapped his hands around both of her upper arms, giving her a little shake. "It damn well is my business. He was my friend, and you're my sister."

"Sean. Stop. You're making me feel sick," she said.

Realizing what he was doing, Sean gasped and instantly

removed his hands from around her arms. "Oh god. I'm so sorry, Emma," he said.

He wasn't really holding or shaking her hard, but her stomach really couldn't handle the jerky movements. But she wasn't about to tell him that, with the way he was acting toward her. Emma gave him a glare, then walked away toward her room, slamming the door and locking it.

She ignored Sean trying to talk to her through her door. Instead, she went into her bathroom, closing and locking that door as well, and turned the water on in the bathtub. She'd take a long soak to calm herself down. She had to think about what had just happened. Once the tub was filled, she sank down into it, sighing at the warmth. Emma was hoping to not think about what just happened, but it was ingrained in her brain and she couldn't stop thinking about it.

Why couldn't her brother have been more supportive? She was so tired of not having anyone on her side. As soon as she thought it, she dismissed it. Noah was supportive of her. He had always been, even when he was frustrated with her.

And what did she do? She broke up with him by voicemail and told him to find out about the baby from the doctor after her appointments.

Who did that to someone who was always making sure she was okay, even when he was as busy as Noah? He worked two jobs—one at the clinic and one at the hospital—and was buying the clinic from the other doctor who wanted to retire.

How many times did he make sure she was eating right and taking breaks at work? He even spent the day with her on his day off to help move all her pottery to the shop. He didn't need to do that.

And now that she was telling herself some more truths, her family and friends would have supported her, too, if she had been brave enough to tell them what was going on.

With Sean being told about them and the baby, it was

probably time for her to step up and tell her family and friends before Sean and his girlfriend did the talking for her.

Once she was done in the bath, she'd call her parents first, then her best friend, Ryleigh. She had been neglecting her friend for the last few weeks, though she had also been busy. They would often go for long stretches without talking when Ryleigh had projects to work on and Emma was deep into her pottery. Then they'd both appear to take a breath and act as though they'd just seen each other yesterday.

But she couldn't wait and had to call her. Not only because she was her friend, but because she was Noah's cousin, too. This baby would be related to her best friend, and she couldn't be happier about it. The word would go out once she told Ryleigh. That was okay.

Emma was stalling on the one person she should be calling first...Noah. She couldn't make herself call him yet. She told herself she'd call him later, after she made the other calls and got herself calmed down from Sean and his anger.

Opening the drain to let some water out, she closed it back up and refilled the tub with more hot water. She'd do it right after she finished her soak.

40

Much later that night, Noah was sitting on his couch blindly watching TV. If someone asked, he wouldn't even be able to say what he was watching. Some sporting event. He looked at the television more closely as it came back from a commercial break. Hmm...looked like rugby. He didn't even like rugby, but it was the only thing on that looked remotely interesting this late at night.

After leaving The Bar with Luke, they went their separate ways. His brother walked in one direction to his apartment, while he went in the other toward his own. He wouldn't be surprised if Luke were still up working on some case from home.

Noah was usually in bed by now. His long days combined with a couple of beers often had him falling asleep as soon as his head hit the pillow. He had the day off tomorrow from both jobs. A rarity for him. Yet he was still going into the clinic early to start working on the hurricane prep.

He needed to make some medical kits with supplies for him, Dr. Mancera, the nurses, and any competent volunteers, like his brother, to take out with them into the field if the hurricane came through like they said it would. If it did, people might be trapped or hurt who needed help. Any injuries they could treat in the field would help to reduce the strain on the hospital, which would need to be cleared for those with more serious injuries.

Even with all of that on his mind, that wasn't why he couldn't sleep. He was still thinking about Emma and what she had said on his voicemail. How was he going to get her back?

Deep in thought, he was startled by his phone ringing. Maybe it was Emma. She couldn't sleep either and had to call to tell him she was kidding about the message she left. Picking up his phone, he was disappointed to see it was Luke.

"Hey, why are you calling so late? Everything all right?" he asked.

"I got a call from Sean," Luke said.

"What? Is it Emma? Is she okay? Let me grab my bag and I'll be right there," he said, starting to panic over the thought that something was wrong with Emma or the baby.

"Noah. Stop. There's nothing wrong with Emma. Sean knows about the two of you and the baby," he explained.

"How did he find out? Did Emma tell him?" He was confused about how he would have found out. She was adamant that Sean was not to find out until she was ready. Did that mean she was ready to tell everyone now?

"I'm not sure how he found out, but it wasn't from Emma. Sean called to warn me that he was going to kill you and wanted me to know so he didn't end up in jail," Luke said, his amusement coming through loud and clear, despite the muffled laugh Noah could hear his twin trying to cover up.

Calling the county sheriff to tell him he was about to kill someone and then expect it to save him from going to jail was not a recommended practice. Sean was obviously not thinking clearly.

"I see our sheriff takes those threats seriously," he said dryly.

"He's not going to actually kill you. Maim you a little...
maybe. Seriously though, he won't be doing anything tonight.
You know Sean. He's going to stew about it overnight and
probably realize it should have been that way all along. He'll
most likely decide he got you two together," his brother said.

"Sure, but in the meantime, I'm not sure I like Emma being
in front of him while he's on a rampage. I can't go over there to
make sure she's all right. Sean would punch first and think
later. I can't get ahold of her...she won't answer her phone. So
swing by their house and make sure she's okay for me, will
you?" he asked.

"I can do that. Emma's carrying my nephew or niece, so I
can make sure she's all right. But if I get punched because Sean
thinks I'm you, then I'm going to be pissed," he said.

"If he does, then arrest him for hitting a police officer or
something. That's a thing, right?" Noah asked.

"It's a thing. Not sure I would blame him or arrest him for it.
I'll just hit him back."

"Good...if he hits you, give him two. One for you and one for
me. Now that I think about it, his girlfriend must have told him
about us and the baby. That he took Marcy's word over
supporting Emma pisses me off," he said.

There was no doubt now that she had heard his
conversation with Emma earlier in his office when she walked
in. That she took that information and told Sean pissed him off
even more. She would not be staying with the clinic once he
was the official owner. He was already thinking about letting
her go for her attitude and lying; now it was personal.

"Will do."

After settling the Sean issue, he and Luke spoke more about
the hurricane and how to coordinate with each other to make
sure they were ready for any injuries during and after
Hurricane Imma.

The storm, pronounced Eem-Ma—and yes, he realized how

close it was to Emma's name—was now a strong CAT four
hurricane and was expected to become stronger before coming
ashore on the west coast of the state late tomorrow night. The
meteorologist said it would run right across the state, coming
out on the east coast.

That meant the eye would come dangerously close to
Cypress Bay as it came through the middle of the state, still as a
significant major hurricane. Noah didn't know why it seemed
all the worst storms that hit Florida began with an 'I'. But he did
know they would be as ready as they could be no matter what
happened during or after the storm.

After the call with Luke, Noah was exhausted. He wouldn't
be able to sleep until he had word from his brother that Emma
was safe, but he needed to be ready to go to bed once he had
word from him. Tomorrow was going to be a long day.

41

Emma made her phone calls that night to her parents and Ryleigh after her bath. The calls were enlightening. She thought her parents would be shocked and her friend would be excited for her. Instead, it was the other way around.

She called her parents first in case Sean decided to take it upon himself to inform them. The first thing her mother said was that it was about time she told them.

"Did Sean call and tell you?" she asked her mother.

"Of course not. You know Sean; he'll rant and rave on his own for a while, then come to his senses, try to fix whatever needs fixing, then he'd come to us to tell us what happened," her mother explained.

"Then how did you know?" Emma asked.

"Did you really think we wouldn't figure it out? By the time you left the house, the day you came over for lunch, we knew exactly what was going on," she said.

"But I just found out that morning!" she exclaimed.

"Amanda went down to the shop to help out when she heard you were going there to drop off your pottery. She wanted to check it out herself. Noah showing up with you was a lucky surprise. Then we compared our suspicions about the two of you and the baby. We've been making plans for when you would both finally tell us ever since," her mother said.

Emma was speechless. She thought they were doing such a good job of keeping everything quiet, but that didn't seem to be the case. Her need to keep it a secret truly was for nothing.

She should have known her mother would have figured it out with the help of Noah's mother. Erica Cooper was best friends with all the Kerrigan women. It started with her and Lauren Kerrigan, who was Simon and Oliver's mother. She recently passed away, and Emma knew her mother was sad not having her around all the time.

Her mother was also best friends with Amanda, the mother of Noah and Luke, and Felicia, the adoptive mother of Hailee. Thinking about the Kerrigan women, the only one her mother had not been friends with was the triplets' mother, Anita, who left their father and the girls when they were still young.

Once she got over her shock, she decided it made no sense to hide anything else. Emma and her mother continued to talk about Noah and the baby, with her mother telling her to make it right with Noah. She knew her mother was right and planned to do just that later—after the storm passed through. There was too much to do in her shop tomorrow morning to prepare for the hurricane that was predicted to come through the next night.

They spent a few more minutes talking about the storm, with her father hopping on to ask whether she or Sean needed any help to put up shutters. They did not because her brother had already finished that before she had come home earlier. Most of what she needed to do at her workshop involved her stock rather than boarding up.

Having hung up with her parents, she called her best friend, Ryleigh, still feeling good about how things went with her parents. She was shocked to realize Ryleigh wouldn't be as receptive as her parents were. She was okay with her seeing her cousin, Noah, but was upset she was just now hearing about the baby.

"Emma, it's not that I'm unhappy for you and Noah. But I'm upset that you felt you couldn't come to me while you were dealing with it all. You didn't need to keep it to yourself. I would have been there for you," Ryleigh said.

"I know, and I'm sorry, but I wasn't ready to tell anyone yet. I've even been holding Noah back from saying anything, even when I knew he was getting frustrated. I wouldn't let him tell anyone," she explained.

"You're forgiven! I could never be mad at you for long, but don't do it again," she said, pretending to be stern and commanding. Ryleigh couldn't pull that off if her life depended on it, so it was laughable. Not that she would laugh at her friend. With her, yes. At her, no.

They spoke a little longer before hanging up. Having everything out in the open was a relief. She didn't think it would be, and now she had something else to apologize to Noah about. She should have agreed with him to tell their families and friends about them and the baby right from the start.

Instead, she made him frustrated with her and both of them upset with each other over what? It wasn't like she would have been able to keep it a secret forever. What would have been the point? She didn't have an answer to that question, and maybe that was for the best.

She would make things right with Noah, but first she had to talk to Sean. Emma couldn't have him going off on her baby's father. It wasn't a good start to either of their relationships with Noah. Or each other.

Stepping out of her room for the first time all night, Emma sought out Sean, finding him in his sunroom art studio. She stood by the open door for a moment, looking at her brother.

He was painting again. Not his usual paintings. No, this was a canvas he reserved for when he was angry, frustrated, or overwhelmed. It was a large canvas that leaned against the wall and allowed him to splatter paint in any way he wanted without a plan or direction. He used it whenever he just needed to vent, allowing him to then move on.

And right now he was smearing paint all over the corner of the large canvas.

"You know, with the direction you're going with your career, it won't be long before everyone will want to buy up every painting you've ever done. I bet this one would still fetch a high price tag one day," she teased her brother.

She wanted to lighten the mood. A serious conversation was a lot easier without him blowing up at her again.

"You might be right," he said calmly.

"Isn't it convenient that you heard about me and Noah and the baby from Marcy? You said she's always asking questions about him. What do you think she's trying to accomplish by telling you about us and the baby? It doesn't make sense," she said, knowing Sean was calm enough to think it through now.

He paused in his painting. "I know you're right. I still don't like it, but it is pretty convenient that I heard about it the way I did."

"There's something about her that I don't really get, Sean."

"I get that," he said, continuing when she gave him a look that said, *then why are you still going out with her.* "I'm not really serious about Marcy and never planned on seeing her for so long. I thought I'd see her for a week or two, have some fun, then move on. You know me. I'm not one to stay in a long-term relationship. But she kept on showing up, and I'm a sucker for a beautiful woman," he explained.

"I wish you would stop telling yourself that. There's more to you than one-night stands and superficial relationships.

Someday there will be someone who knocks you off your feet, and you won't know what to do about it," she told him.

"Once again, you're probably right," he admitted with a sigh.

"I'm afraid, Sean. That's why I didn't want anyone to know about me and Noah, or the baby. I used the excuse that I was worried about what you would say or do to stop him from telling everyone from the beginning. But I know you'd be happy for me if I were happy," she said.

"What are you really afraid of, Emma?" he asked.

"That Noah will realize I'm not worth the little time he has to spend with me. He's a busy man. Why would he want to spend time with me, someone who is barely making it with my pottery, and despite that, spends all my time holed up in my workshop? And now we're having a baby. What will happen if I'm stuck in my head in a project and forget about him or her? I just don't feel ready," she confessed.

"Emma, you aren't going to forget about your baby. And you have more than enough people around to help out, too. As for Noah, there is no way he does not think you're worth it. He's been in love with you for a long time," Sean said.

"He has? Then why were you angry when you found out about us?" she asked.

"I wasn't angry that you were dating each other. I was angry that I had to find out from Marcy. You both should have told me, but Noah should have come to me himself and told me right away. I didn't know you told him not to say anything. I thought he was trying to keep it from me. That's why I was angry," he said.

"I love him. I hoped we could be a family, but I said some not so nice things and told him to take a hike."

"I don't think you'll have any problems getting him back. And if anyone is good enough for my sister, I guess Noah would be the best man for you that I know," he told her.

"I planned on talking to him after this storm comes through. Maybe everything will be all right. Oh, and I called Mom and Dad already. So you don't need to go blabbing to them now," she said as she walked out of his studio.

Sean followed her out when the doorbell rang. Who would be coming by this late at night?

Her brother looked through the peephole and swore before unlocking and opening the door. "What are you doing here?" he asked harshly.

"Just checking up on things. Everything all right here, Emma?" Luke asked.

Why would Luke be asking her if she was all right? "Of course, why wouldn't I be?" she answered with a question of her own.

"Oh, no reason," he said. "Have a good night."

Luke turned around and walked back to his patrol car, got in and drove away.

"What was that all about?"

"Nothing. Don't worry about it," Sean said, closing the door when Luke's car disappeared around the corner.

Whatever was going on, she wasn't sure she wanted to know. For now, she just wanted to go to bed. It was a long day, and tomorrow was looking to be even longer with all the work she needed to do before the storm hit. Walking away from her brother, she told him goodnight over her shoulder and went into her bedroom, closing and locking the door.

42

Early the next morning, Noah was at the clinic doing the final, last-minute preparations for Hurricane Imma. They hired some locals to board the place up already, but Noah still needed to organize the supplies into kits in case they needed to take care of people out in the neighborhoods after the storm.

The clinic was officially closed today because of the storm, but they decided to have at least one doctor at the clinic during regular business hours, in case there were any emergencies. They didn't need their full staff today—one doctor could take care of any minor emergencies on his own—and that would allow their employees to do their own preparations and to find a safe place to ride out the storm.

Appointments were rescheduled, and any major emergencies would be directed to the hospital, either transported on their own or by ambulance.

He was taking the morning shift, while Dr. Mancera would be by in the afternoon. Noah would close the place up and make sure it was locked up tight for the hurricane expected to come through that night. It was a monster storm. He was hoping the clinic would still be in one piece by the time it was done.

Leaving the front door locked with a sign to ring the bell for emergencies, he walked back to the storage closet and began taking a quick inventory. He brought some small packs for supplies with straps that fit across the body to keep their hands free as they were going from patient to patient. Noah really hoped it wouldn't come to that, though. He would rather spend all this time preparing them for nothing. The thought of why he would need them and the destruction it would mean left him with a bad feeling.

Finished stuffing some of the bags with supplies, he left the supply closet to bring them to the front. He would put a bunch of them in his car so he had them available if needed. Closing the closet door, he turned and saw Sean walking down the hallway.

"Hey...what are you doing here? And more importantly, how did you get in?" Noah asked him.

"The door was unlocked and propped open. I looked for you at your apartment, and when I didn't find you there, I figured you'd be here," Sean explained as he walked up to him.

Sean leaned against the wall, his hands in his pockets. He supposed that meant his friend hadn't come to beat him up. That was progress anyway.

Noah still looked at him nervously. Who knew if he was just trying to get him to relax before deciding to punch him? His friend was sneaky that way. "Okay. And now you've found me."

"I know you've been seeing Emma and that she's pregnant," he said.

"And let me guess, you're here to kill me over it."

Sean chuckled. "If I found you last night, then probably. But after talking it out with Emma and sleeping on it, there is no one I'd rather have with her than you."

Noah was surprised by Sean's quick turnaround. In the

past, he was the one to hold grudges the longest—especially if someone messed with his sister.

"Thanks for being supportive, man. I love Emma, if she wanted me, that is, but she doesn't want anything to do with me anymore," he said, feeling lower than he had in a long time. If it weren't for the hurricane bearing down on them, he'd go wherever she was and stay put until she talked to him. But this was the worst possible time, and he was worried that giving her more time to stew would make it harder for him to get her back.

"I don't think that's true. Just go to her and I'm sure everything will work out fine. The real problem we have now is Marcy. She's the one who told me about you, Emma, and the baby," he growled.

That bitch! Noah was not someone who disparaged or called women names. He was raised better than that, but this woman was doing everything possible to mess with his friends and family. That was where he drew the line between being polite and letting what little temper he had out.

"I had already planned on firing her once I took over the clinic. Unfortunately, there's not much I can do until that happens. Dr. Mancera is in charge, and he does all the hiring and firing. I've mentioned the issues with her to him before, but he doesn't seem inclined to do anything about it.

"I have other concerns about her. Nothing illegal that I know of, but her unprofessional attitude around the patients, obvious lying, and hanging out at the clinic when she's not scheduled to work is suspicious, too," Noah told him.

He'd found her in the hallways of the clinic more than a few times when she wasn't supposed to be working. He wasn't sure what she was doing at the clinic—nothing seemed to be missing or moved around. But it was a busy clinic with a lot of supplies, offices, rooms, and people. Noah didn't know where everything was at all times. For all he knew, she was stealing from them as well. He couldn't prove it, though.

"Well, as much as I'd like to confront her about it right now, this hurricane coming in has more of my attention," Sean said. "I have the house all boarded up, including shutters around my studio. Damn place looks like a cave. But I still want to move my paintings up off the floor and into an interior room in case we have any flooding or damage."

"Is Emma's workshop all secure? Does she need anything else done?" Noah couldn't help but ask. She may have broken up with him, but he loved her, and she was carrying his baby. The last thing he wanted was for either of them to be unsafe in this storm.

"She told me this morning that she had a couple more things to secure in her workshop, then she's coming home and will be staying put for the storm with me," he said.

"Good. Keep an eye on her for me, Sean."

"You know I will. I'm going to make a quick stop before heading home to do that last-minute hurricane prep," he said as he walked down the hallway toward the bathrooms at the front of the clinic.

Grabbing the medical kits, Noah followed him toward the front of the clinic. On his way there, he remembered what Sean had said when he had asked him how he got inside. His friend told him the door was open and propped up. But that couldn't be. He remembered closing and locking the door, putting the sign outside that said to ring the bell for service. No one should have been able to come in without him unlocking it.

Hurrying down the hall, he put the bags down on the front desk. The clinic waiting room was dark and bleak. The only lights on were those above the front desk, where Allison sat. All the windows were covered with plywood, giving an eerie, closed-in feel to the space, with the glass door the only area not yet covered. Sid had someone ready to put that last piece of plywood up after Noah locked up for the night.

Sean was right. The front door to the clinic wasn't wide open, but it was opened a crack with a sliver of wood stuck in the bottom of the door.

Someone else was in the clinic.

A noise came from behind him down the other hallway. Thinking it might be Sean, he turned to tell him about his find. Instead, Marcy was coming from the hall that led to the patient rooms, her head down, looking at some supplies she had in her hand.

"Did you find what you were looking for, Marcy?" he growled.

Her head shot up in shock, and she looked at him with a panicked look on her face for a moment before it disappeared and was replaced with a smile.

"There you are, Noah. I was looking for you." Her eyes darted over to the front desk where he put the medical kit bags. "I came by to see if you needed any help to get ready for the hurricane."

"I don't need any help. Here, I'll take those supplies," he said, taking the supplies out of her hands. "You should go home and take care of your own preparations."

"Oh, I'm all done. That's why I came here. To help you," she said, starting to walk closer to him.

"I do have a question for you, Marcy. Hear anything interesting lately? About me and Sean's sister maybe?" he asked.

That stopped her in her tracks. "What do you mean?" she asked. She looked nervous. Marcy was wringing her hands together as though they'd gone damp and she had to wipe them off.

It was at this moment that Sean walked out of the bathroom. "Well, Marcy. Interesting seeing you here. I thought you said last night you were going to Orlando this morning to ride out the storm with your parents," he said, catching her in another lie.

"Oh, was that the plan, Marcy?" Noah picked up. So she got caught in another lie. That wasn't surprising to him.

"Of course! And it's still the plan. I just thought I'd come by to see if Dr. Kerrigan needed any help before I left," she stuttered out.

"It's Dr. Kerrigan now, huh?" Sean began. "Last night and any other time we went out, come to think of it, you called him Noah. Now that he's right in front of us, he's Dr. Kerrigan. Interesting."

Sean wasn't one to let things go. Noah was going to let him handle this the way he saw fit. His friend would do a much better job as the boyfriend than he could as the soon-to-be boss. At least until he became the boss, and he fired her.

"Well, we're in the clinic now, so I need to be professional," she said.

Noah snorted lightly. She was never professional at the clinic. Why Marcy was suddenly acting like it mattered now with no one else around, he'd never understand.

"It wasn't very professional to gossip about Noah and my sister to me last night. Was it?" he bit out.

"I don't know what you're talking about," she said.

The woman had a death wish. Lying to him was one thing. Noah wasn't one to hold grudges. He was pissed at her earlier when he found out she was talking about him, Emma, and the baby.

But now that things were good with Sean, it wasn't worth it to keep that anger inside. Sean, on the other hand, did hold grudges. She wouldn't be coming out of this in one piece by the time he was done with her. It may not be today, but someday Marcy would wish she hadn't played these games with him.

In the meantime, they really didn't have time for this anymore.

"Why don't you go and head down to Orlando? This can be solved later after the storm," he told her. It was also said for Sean's benefit. The last thing he needed was for Sean to get all riled up over this woman and what she did. With a major hurricane bearing down on them, their preparations had to come first.

"Yes, of course," she said before walking out the door.

"We're good, Sean. Let it go for now. She'll get what she deserves later," he told his friend.

"I know you're right, but it pisses me off that I let that go on for way too long," his friend said before leaving the clinic, too.

Noah picked up the medical kit bags and walked over to the door, turning over the sign to tell anyone who came by they were out with a number to call in an emergency. Kicking the wood sliver out from the door, he let it close and lock behind him.

His mind already off the confrontation with his nurse, he placed the bags into his car and decided to see if Emma needed any help in her workshop.

Marcy was pissed that Noah couldn't see they would be great together. And he and Sean confronted her, telling her they didn't appreciate her butting into their lives like she did.

Screw them all!

She'd destroy them, and then they'd see they shouldn't have messed with her. Noah should have realized that girl was no good for him. Sean should have been mad at his sister for sleeping with his best friend. Then Noah would have realized he couldn't live without Marcy.

But did that happen? No!

She knew just how she'd pay them back. First, she'd take care of the clinic, then she'd take care of the girl.

Standing around the corner of the clinic, Marcy waited until Noah and Sean left. What they didn't realize was she had made a copy of Dr. Mancera's key. Marcy had access to come and go as she pleased. And frequently did.

After waiting a few minutes more to make sure no one came back, the nurse walked to the front door and unlocked it, slipping inside.

Now they'd see what happened for scolding her!

43

The sound of the door unlocking reached her as Emma finished placing some of her pottery into crates. She had to secure what she could to prepare for the hurricane that was slated to come through later that night.

She'd bet her parents or Sean showed up to assist even though Emma told them there wasn't much left to do.

Instead, Noah walked in. He was the last person she thought she'd see today. Not that she wasn't happy to see him. She did want to make things right, but with all the storm prep happening, she resigned herself to not seeing him until after the storm passed by.

Emma cautiously asked, "What are you doing here?" She hadn't spoken to him since their break up by voicemail yesterday.

Not saying a word, he walked over to her and cupped her face with his hands. "There is nothing you could say that would prevent me from making sure you and the baby were all right."

Stepping away from Noah, she was disappointed. She hoped he would say he loved her. Not that he came by to take care of her because of the baby. If he was put off by her reaction, he didn't say anything.

"Is there anything I can do to help?" he asked.

"I just need to pack up all the completed pottery, then decide what to do about those that are not fired yet." Emma looked around her workshop. She had a lot of finished pieces in crates already, but thankfully she didn't have as much as usual since she dropped off that shipment to the shop with Noah's help.

"What would happen if they were not fired up yet?" Noah asked.

"They would become deformed if I tried to pack them that way. It would be better to either try to fire up the rest before the storm, or just leave them out and take the chance of them getting ruined."

More than half of the workshop held shelves full of unfinished work. She didn't know if she would be able to save them all if something happened to the workshop in the storm. The pottery that was already fired but still incomplete would most likely survive. Crating those up gave them extra protection.

But the pieces that were still drying on the shelves waiting to be fired had to stay on the shelves. It was a risk, but one she had to take. Some were ready to be fired in the kiln—she had some already in it—and she would continue to add to them for as long as she had before the workshop had to be closed up for the storm.

Anything in the ovens should be able to stay inside, as long as they were done, and the ovens were turned off before the hurricane hit. She couldn't risk the whole place burning down. Who knew what would happen if one of them were tipped over or something crashed on top of them?

Thankfully, there wasn't anything to prep other than the pottery. The building was as secure as possible. There were no windows in the workshop, and the whole thing was made of metal, steel beams framing it all in, with metal siding and roof. It wasn't indestructible, though. The doors were the weakest point, so she had someone come by earlier and put up the metal shutters she had to secure the garage door. As long as the roof held up, everything should be fine. If not, then she'd have a long clean-up.

Nothing left was worth more than her and her baby's lives though. So she'd ride out the storm at the house with Sean. If she found any damage to the workshop, as much as it would pain her, she'd clean up after the storm and recreate anything damaged.

"I can pack up the rest of your completed pottery while you continue firing up the ones that need it," he suggested.

Emma agreed, and they got to work. Once done packing, Noah helped her with the rest—under her direct instructions on what to do.

"There's not much else we can do right now. The pottery needs to stay in the oven for a bit," she said.

"I can stay with you until you're ready to leave," he said.

"No, that's okay. I'm not staying much longer. I'll clean up this mess, then I'll go home to stay with Sean," she told him.

Noah kissed Emma on the forehead. "Stay safe and call me if you need anything. We'll talk after the storm."

She nodded in agreement. Wanting to go home soon, Emma got back to work once he left, the door locking behind him.

44

Noah headed back to the clinic to make a few more medical kits. The ones he made earlier were in his car, so they would be ready to go in case he needed to travel or pass them off to others to help. But they always needed more. He'd stock up the patient rooms and see if Dr. Mancera was at the clinic yet.

As he drove, he couldn't help thinking about Emma. It wouldn't be easy to win her back, but it seemed insurmountable to be able to do it while also dealing with a hurricane about to bear down on them.

Noah noticed Sid's car was not in the parking lot as he arrived at the clinic. Guess it was just him for now, he thought. Of course, that would be the case soon, once the paperwork was all signed and notarized in a few short weeks. He would be busy trying to find another doctor to join him at his clinic.

His clinic.

That still left him with a feeling of awe. He would own the clinic soon. While it made him nervous to think about, he was also excited to be able to put his own plans for the clinic into motion.

Walking up to the front, the door was unlocked. Noah had locked it after he and Sean had left this morning. Maybe Sid did show up. He might have parked his car behind the clinic or had someone drop him off. That would explain why he didn't see his car, and the door was unlocked. He didn't want to think about any other explanations yet.

"Sid! You in here?" Noah called out to the older doctor. He didn't hear anyone respond, and that had him concerned.

He walked through the clinic. Maybe Dr. Mancera was in his office with the door closed or seeing a patient in one of the rooms.

As he walked back to the offices and patient rooms on Sid's side of the clinic, he noticed all the doors were open and the rooms empty. Maybe he was in the supply closet or working on Noah's side of the building?

Down the other hallway, on his side of the clinic, everything was trashed. The supply room door was open, with supplies torn apart. In his patient rooms, everything on the counters was scattered in piles on the floor.

He walked to his office and saw that it was also a disaster. With papers strewn all over the desk and floor, his chair upended. He couldn't believe what he was seeing, but he knew exactly who had done it.

Marcy.

Taking out his cell phone, he clicked on his brother's name. "Hey, can you stop by the clinic? Someone trashed the place."

After getting a quick affirmative from his twin, he hung up and called Sean to warn him to be careful. It seemed as though Marcy was not happy with them. Just what he needed before a major storm hit.

Good thing he had those medical kits in his car or they would be hurting for supplies if anyone was injured from the storm. Noah was even more pissed as he thought about who might not receive help because Marcy had decided to exact revenge on the much-needed supplies. He'd need to do a complete inventory after Luke investigated to see what could be salvaged and what was a loss.

"Noah!" his brother called out from the front of the clinic.

"Back here in the hallway on the right," he yelled back.

Luke turned the corner into the hallway, with a deputy following close behind. His twin stopped in his tracks when he saw the destruction in front of him.

"What the hell," he muttered.

"Exactly what I thought. It's all the way down this hallway, coming out of the supply closet on the left, in the patient rooms, and in my office. Dr. Mancera's hallway and office are fine, by the way," he told him.

"Someone has a vendetta against you, brother."

Noah snorted out a dry chuckle. "No shit."

"This doesn't look like Sean's style. Want to tell me what's been going on?"

"No, it definitely wasn't Sean," he said, delving into the story of what happened from the time he last spoke with Luke late last night until when he just walked into the clinic again, finding the mess left all over his hallway and rooms.

"Damn. This is the last thing I need today with that hurricane about to hit," Luke sighed. "Okay, we need to get in here and document the mess. Call in who we need for that, Pedro, and have dispatch send a deputy to see if they can find the woman and question where she was during the time Noah said she'd be here."

Luke was all business now. He went from relaxed to stone-cold in a second.

"Do you want them to take fingerprints?" Pedro asked.

"Yes. Have them do it to rule out anyone else. It won't help otherwise since she's a nurse here. Her prints should be everywhere, anyway."

"Not in my office," Noah added. "Sure, her prints may be on some of the paperwork, but there should be no reason for any prints other than my own behind my desk."

"Good point. Have them pay close attention to getting prints on the desk drawer pulls, chair and anything else only Noah would touch," Luke commanded.

The deputy nodded and walked away to make the calls to dispatch.

"I'm sorry, but you can't clean up anything yet," he told his brother.

"I know. Damn it! She knew we needed these supplies after the storm came through to help with injuries. It pisses me off that this was how she'd come at me. This isn't just about me; this affects the whole town. She knew exactly where to hit us where it would hurt the most."

"Maybe some can be salvaged, but you won't have much time before the storm is here. It sped up, Noah. We only have a few hours before the outer rainbands reach us; the worst of them may contain tornadic activity at sunset. Instead of the hurricane coming through overnight, it'll be here about dinner time. They said the eye will pass just north of us and Noah...it's expected to remain a CAT four when it comes through," Luke explained gravely.

That wasn't good. It meant they not only had less time to make final preparations, but the town would be in the right-front quadrant of the storm. Not the best place to be. The destruction was going to be immense.

The only saving grace was how fast it was moving. It didn't give the storm time to break apart, so would keep its intensity, but it also meant it wouldn't sit over the town wreaking havoc for a long period of time. Hurricane Imma would move through fast, destroy what it wanted to destroy, then move on. They'd be left cleaning up the mess.

"Okay then," he started, resigned at what was to come. "Let

me know when you're done here and I'll go through what I can of the supplies. I can wait to clean up my office, but we'll need whatever supplies we can get our hands on. I'll start pulling whatever I can from Sid's side while you're doing what you need to do over here," Noah said as he walked away.

45

After doing everything possible to save her stock, Emma went home and decided to take a little nap before going back to the workshop to take care of the ovens before the storm arrived. She'd rest for an hour, go back to the workshop, spend another hour finishing up, then she had plenty of time to get back home before the storm hit.

She was getting tired so quickly these days. Must be because of the pregnancy, she thought. As she was lying on her bed about to fall asleep, Emma put her hand on her slightly bulging stomach. "Everything will be fine, baby. I love your father, and even if we're not together, even if he doesn't love me, we will both love and be there for you." Lying down on her bed, she covered herself up with her comforter and fell instantly asleep.

Hours later, she lurched up in her bed. Looking around, she couldn't figure out why it was already so dark. The room had already been darker than usual because of the boards Sean had put up on the windows, but some light had peaked through the edges, which provided the room with a sliver of light. That light was no longer showing through.

Had she slept more than she wanted to? It seemed like it was just for a minute, but after glancing at the clock she realized she'd been sleeping for two hours instead of just the one-hour nap she wanted.

She had no choice. Emma couldn't leave the ovens on when the storm whipped through Cypress Bay. She'd just be quick...run over to the shop, turn off the ovens, then come right back to the house to hunker down. She should have more than enough time before the storm approached. It wasn't supposed to come through for at least another five or more hours.

Leaving her room, she didn't see Sean in any of their common areas of their home. He must be in his studio or room, she thought. Not wanting to bother him, she went out the door without telling him she was leaving. It wasn't like she'd be gone for long.

The sky was starting to become a little dark, just like in her room. Figuring it was one of the very outer rainbands, she kept on driving until she reached the workshop. They weren't usually any worse than a normal rainstorm.

When she pulled into her parking space, Emma realized something was not right. The door to the workshop was propped open. Her first thought was that maybe her brother wasn't at home after all and was instead in her workshop. How dare he come to check up on her preparations! He was always treating her as though she weren't an adult or able to take care of things for herself. Not thinking about her own safety, Emma went storming inside expecting to catch Sean double-checking her storm preparations.

"If you think you can come in here and do a better job of prepping for the storm than I can, then you have no idea who you're dealing with, Sean! I'm not going to put up with your high-handed crap anymore!" she yelled as she walked all the way into the middle of the workshop.

He was always acting as though she was still a little child

that he had to watch out for. That was part of the reason she didn't want to tell him about her relationship with Noah or the baby.

Now that she got that all out, she looked around for Sean. Instead of catching him messing with her stuff, she saw his girlfriend, Marcy. She couldn't process what she was seeing. The woman was standing next to one of the shelves, where she had left some unfinished work, a pile of broken, unfired pottery at her feet.

"What are you doing in my workshop?" Emma asked the woman.

"Noah should have been mine. But he rejected me because of you! It's all your fault! Once you're out of his life, then he'll realize I was meant to be his all along," she said, spouting out her hatred toward her.

Emma was horrified and noticed the woman had also opened up one of her crates and smashed her completed pottery on the floor. The bitch!

"You can't get away with this. I'm calling the sheriff's office. If you don't leave right now, I'll press charges and you'll go to jail," she told the crazy woman. Emma took out her phone, prepared to call Luke.

Marcy screamed and ran at Emma. She tried to move out of the way of the woman coming at her, but it was not enough. When the woman approached, she wrapped her arms around Emma, tackling her.

They crashed into one of the shelving units filled with smaller crates. Emma was unable to stop their momentum completely. Shelves and crates began to topple over, colliding with the pair as they all fell inward toward the concrete floor.

The other woman made contact first, the shelving unit and crates hitting her head and body. She fell to the ground, her head bouncing off the concrete floor, knocking her out.

Emma twisted away from the falling debris, but wasn't able

to avoid it. The heavy shelving unit and crates hit her in the shoulder and side, causing her to scream out in pain and fall to the concrete ground.

With everything surrounding them, Marcy was now completely covered by the shelving unit, crates, and broken pottery. Emma was only slightly better, being only partially covered by the same debris.

The phone fell out of her hand. As she attempted to reach out for it, she noticed the wind and rain picking up outside the open door. Crap, the storm already arrived. And with the door open, that meant the heavy winds would come inside and tear her workshop apart.

Shit! She was in big trouble. She hurt all over, her head spinning, making it hard to focus on anything around her. Emma tried to move out from under the debris on top of her, but with the first move she made, pain shot through her body.

The movement was enough to shift another precariously leaning shelving unit, causing a small crate on top to fall off. Instantly reacting, she cradled her stomach and hunched over herself as much as possible to protect the baby inside.

Bouncing off another larger crate, the smaller one hit Emma on the side of the head. Her last thought before passing out...a hope her baby would survive.

46

Noah was hunkered down at the clinic, waiting for the storm to pass. He couldn't be at his apartment since it was on the second floor of the building, all the windows were boarded up. His parents' company hired others to take care of all their buildings whenever hurricanes came through.

Not that they've ever had one as strong as Hurricane Imma in the last decade, even close to Cypress Bay. They had been lucky, but that luck had run out. It was now bearing down on them. The first squall lines came through in waves, and they were now getting wider and wider as the storm came closer.

With the clinic being a one-story concrete block building, it was the perfect place to wait out the storm. The windows in the waiting room and those in their offices were all boarded up, including the front door.

The back door they used for supply deliveries was available to enter and leave the building if needed. It was a steel core door with a double lock and didn't need to be boarded up. He only hoped that no debris from the storm blocked his only way out. Then he'd need to wait until Luke came to release him from the front.

225

While he waited for the storm to pass, Noah continued to clean up the mess his nurse—no former nurse—Marcy made of their supplies. Thankfully, only a small handful of the much-needed supplies were ruined. She was lucky it wasn't more. She was already going to jail for what she did.

When he told Dr. Mancera what happened later that afternoon, he was shocked and apologetic for not taking what Noah had told him about her bad behavior seriously and doing something about it sooner. The older doctor was tired after an already full day of prepping his own house for the storm, that he told him to go home.

He'd stay at the clinic, clean up and make sure everything was safe with the building. Sid didn't even try to refuse his offer, thanking him and saying he'd see Noah after the storm before walking out the front door.

As he finished cleaning up one of the exam rooms, his phone trilled out with an incoming call. Looking at the phone, he saw Sean's name come up. He probably wanted to see what was going on with Marcy.

Good, that meant he could find out what Emma was doing during the storm. Have Sean check on her and their baby to make sure she had everything they needed. It felt good to be able to talk openly about them and the baby. He didn't realize how tense he had been all this time, not being able to say anything, until all the tension went away.

"Hey, Sean. Everything good at your house?" he said as he answered the phone.

"Noah. I can't find Emma. I thought she was at home taking a nap. When I didn't hear or see her for a while, I peeked into her room. It was empty. I checked for her car and it was gone too. Noah, I'm worried Emma didn't realize the storm was coming sooner and went to her workshop," Sean said frantically.

Every muscle in Noah's body tensed up again with fear for

Emma. He thought back to their conversation at her workshop earlier that day and realized they never spoke about how the hurricane was speeding up and would be arriving sooner than they thought.

He didn't think to mention it because she'd already told him she was only staying for another hour. Noah thought she'd be safe at home with Sean and didn't bother to tell her. And now she may be at her workshop. Granted it was well constructed, but it wasn't category four hurricane strong.

"Stay home in case she calls or comes back. I'll go see if she's at her workshop," he told his friend.

Running to the back of the clinic, he unlocked the back door and went outside into a deluge. He was instantly soaked through from the rain. The wind was already starting to pick up to the point that it was almost too hard for him to shut the back door.

He ran to his car, thankful he had the medical kits in it. He didn't know what he'd find at Emma's workshop. He was worried they wouldn't be able to leave once he arrived, but he'd be damned if anyone thought he would leave her at the workshop by herself.

The storm was blowing small debris and rain all around him. Using all his strength, he closed his car door and started up the engine, putting it into gear before driving off toward the workshop and his future.

Throughout the entire way, he fought to keep his car on the road. Roof shingles and branches were already being thrown around by the wind, and he hoped he'd make it to the workshop without getting hit by anything bigger. Noah couldn't lose Emma. She had to be all right.

Pulling up to the steel structure, he caught two things right away. The first was Emma's Mini Cooper sitting out in the open like a sore thumb. She'd be lucky it wasn't smashed to pieces by the time this storm was over.

The second was the open door swinging wildly back and forth against the side of the workshop. She knew to close everything up. Leaving any kind of opening invited the wind in, almost guaranteeing the wind would whip around inside and help tear off the roof.

And because she knew it, his thoughts immediately segued into something being wrong. She just wouldn't leave the door open. Ever, but especially during a hurricane.

Noah grabbed one of the medical kits before struggling to open the car door, the wind slamming it closed behind him. Not bothering to lock it, he raced inside, grabbing the workshop door and closing it on his way in. Anything to prevent any more damage. Once he knew Emma was safe, he was going to make sure she knew how upset he was that she had put herself and their baby in this kind of danger.

Looking around the inside of the workshop, he couldn't take in what it looked like. When he had left earlier that day, it had been a little cluttered with crates stacked along the outer walls, but this was a mess. Pieces of pottery lie scattered and broken all over the floor. Metal shelves were tipped over. What he didn't see was Emma, and that scared him the most.

"Emma!" he yelled over the howling wind.

He received no response, but he thought he heard a low moan coming from the other side of the workshop. It could have been the wind; he really didn't know. The workshop wasn't closed in, so if she was here, the only other place to hide where he couldn't see her was the bathroom. He rushed over to the small half-bath sitting in the corner of the large room. Peeking inside, he found it empty.

"Emma!" he tried once more.

"Noah. Help," he heard softly from his left.

Rushing over to where he heard her, he was shocked to see a shelving unit and smaller crates scattered on and around Emma, who was lying motionless on the floor.

"Emma, are you all right? Where does it hurt?" he asked her frantically. This could not be happening.

"I don't know. I'm not sure. Everything fell on me when she attacked me. I feel kind of numb everywhere," she told him.

He looked over her and the situation. Her head was bleeding, but not excessively. She had a lot of blood down the side of her face, so he imagined it had bled a lot at first and was already slowing down. That might mean she had been lying on the floor for some time.

The shelving unit was lying partially on her side and shoulder. Her hands were cradling her stomach. Noah couldn't think about the baby right now. He had to concentrate on getting Emma out of the debris and somewhere safer to ride out the storm. Trying to figure out the best way to move the debris off her, he thought back to what she said. Someone attacked her.

"Who else is here, Emma? You said she attacked you. Who did this?" he asked.

"Marcy. She was here wrecking my pottery. She rushed me, and we crashed into the shelves. Everything started coming down. She's hurt. You need to go check on her," Emma gasped.

Wrecking the clinic wasn't enough for the woman? She had to come here and attack his girlfriend, too. No, he wouldn't be rushing to help her until he made sure Emma was safe. "Let me take care of you, then I'll check on her. We can't stay in the middle of the workshop. The storm's here, and we need to find somewhere safe to wait it out," he told her. Moving around some of the crates, he said, "Tell me if anything hurts too much."

Noah continued to move all the crates from on top of and around Emma. His whole body clenched every time she moaned. Finally, everything other than the shelving unit was cleared away from the area. "Okay, I'm going to lift the shelf off you. Do you think you can crawl out from underneath it, or do you need some help?"

"I can do it," she said.

"On three. One. Two. Three." He lifted the shelf, giving just enough room for Emma to scoot herself out from underneath. Once she was out of the way, Noah put it back down before rushing back over to her.

"What hurts?"

"I'm good, Noah. A little sore, but I don't know how long I've been under the shelf. Something hit my head, and I think I passed out," she said.

Damn. He knew the cut on her head couldn't have been fresh, but it wasn't good that she passed out after getting hit. Noah was hoping she would tell him she had scraped it on something. Though now that he really looked at it, he saw a knot on the side of her head, too.

"As soon as we get out of here, I'm bringing you to the hospital. I want you and the baby to get a full check-up. Now we need to get to the bathroom. It's a smaller area, and we'll be safer from falling or flying debris."

"What about Marcy? And my kilns are still on. I need to turn them off."

"I'm going to get you somewhere safe first, then I'll turn off the ovens and check on Marcy," he told her. "Tell me if I hurt you when I lift you up."

Tucking one arm under her legs and the other behind her back, Noah gently lifted her up off the floor. She gave another moan at the movement, closing her eyes. It was most likely to stave off any dizziness from the hit on her head. He didn't want to hurt her more than she already was, but he couldn't leave her there. Hurrying to the back of the workshop, he entered the small bathroom and gently placed her on the floor next to the pedestal sink.

"Wrap yourself around this. You can lean on the pedestal or

the wall if you need to. I'll go check on Marcy and turn off the ovens. I'll be back in a minute."

Moving fast now, Noah ran to the ovens and switched them off. That done, he went back to where Emma told him Marcy might be located. The pile of crates was bigger here along with another shelving unit. Moving some of the items, he found Marcy lying motionless under the pile.

A large pool of blood rested under her head, and he already knew it wasn't good. Leaning over the crates, he placed his fingers on her neck to check for a pulse. Nothing. He suspected she had died the instant her head had hit the concrete.

Unable to do anything else for her now, Noah had to leave her until after the storm. His first priority was to keep Emma, the baby, and himself safe as the hurricane passed through.

He saw the medical kit he had dropped. Scooping it up, he rushed back to the bathroom, closing the door to help keep them protected.

47

Emma was scared. She never planned on riding out the hurricane in her workshop. It wasn't really set up to sustain itself as a shelter. She felt the wind pushing against the walls of the workshop, heard the whistling of the wind, and the pounding of the rain on the roof.

Noah had left her a few minutes ago to turn off her ovens and check on Marcy. She still couldn't believe that the woman who was dating her brother had come into her workshop to wreck her stock and attack her.

It was crazy!

She was so deep in thought, clinging to the pedestal of the sink, that she didn't hear Noah come back into the bathroom. The door slamming shut snapped her out of her thoughts.

She looked up at him expectantly. Emma thought he'd bring Marcy in with him. She may be batshit crazy, but no one deserved to be left out in the workshop during a storm of this magnitude.

He looked down at her and shook his head. She knew what that meant...the woman hadn't made it. The thought made her sad for a moment until she thought about how she wouldn't be hurt right now if it weren't for her.

Sure she probably would have still been at her workshop during the storm—she admitted it wasn't the greatest of decisions she'd ever made—but she wouldn't have had crates and shelves fall on her if the woman hadn't been in her shop.

He moved and sat down behind Emma, wrapping himself around her, his arms cocooning her and his hands covering her own. She felt a great weight lift. She wasn't alone in riding out the storm anymore.

Everything around them was shaking. One minute felt like an hour. Emma knew now that the storm was moving through at a fast speed, but it felt like it would never end. Her workshop was one of the worst places to ride out the storm. On top of that, she hurt.

Emma didn't want to worry Noah more than he already was. She'd tell him after they got through this storm. But her whole body hurt, and her stomach felt like it was cramping. She was so worried about losing the baby. Emma may have been surprised about the pregnancy, but she could not deny any longer that she loved her baby more than anything.

Losing the baby would devastate her. And another thing she realized was how much she loved Noah. If she lost the baby, would he not want her anymore? When she thought of losing him...well, it might break her completely.

All these thoughts about loss made her remember that Marcy was lying dead on the other side of her workshop. Emma was sorry the woman was dead. She didn't deserve to die. But the woman would have killed her and her baby. And for what? Because she wanted Noah? It was unreal. Marcy never had him to begin with, and she was dating Emma's brother, Sean.

The howling winds picked up speed, indicating they were in the thick of the storm. The rain was pounding on the metal roof. It was so loud that Noah's whispered words in her ear that everything would be all right as they tightly gripped the sink pedestal were whisked away in the roar.

A large bang against the side of the workshop reverberated throughout the building, causing Emma to scream out in fright. Wind whistled through what was most probably a hole of some kind in the side of the building. She could only imagine what hit the building to create it. The pressure became intense as the storm continued.

A horrible screeching from the far corner of the workshop near the front door had Emma jump and scream. It sounded like part of the roof tore away from the steel structure, exposing the area by the door to the elements and rushing wind. The metal roofing banged like a drumbeat over and over in the wind against the steel beams.

It was more disconcerting to her that she couldn't actually see what was going on with the building and all her pottery. With the bathroom door shut tight and no windows, they were blind to everything happening around them.

The sounds, though, were enough for her to understand that what was happening would not be good in the end. Her workshop was most likely destroyed. But she couldn't think about that now. They had to make it through this storm alive. That was all that mattered.

What seemed like days later, but was really only hours, Emma heard the storm begin to die down. Noah was still whispering in her ear that they were going to make it. She didn't know if he was trying to reassure her or himself, but she was thankful he was with her. Her whole body was tense and tight. She'd be sore all over when this was done.

"Hold on a little longer, sweetheart," she heard him whisper. Emma wasn't sure if she could hold on anymore. Her head hurt, and she was lightheaded and dizzy again. She was so tired and wanted to rest, but she couldn't yet. The adrenaline running through her body allowed her to stay awake, though she would have passed out ages ago without it.

Another hour later, the winds were no more than a light breeze and the banging of the roof stopped. She started to relax for the first time in hours. All the tension and adrenaline drained out, leaving her limp and tired. The last thing she remembered was Noah removing his arms from around the pedestal. He was saying something to her, but she couldn't make it out as she drifted off.

48

Slowly unwrapping himself from around Emma, Noah felt her go limp in his arms. Looking down at her, he saw she had passed out once more. An adrenaline drop might be responsible, but she also had the head wound and who knew what else. He had to get them out of the workshop and her to the hospital.

Placing her gently on the ground, Noah walked over to the bathroom door and pulled it open. Peering out into the workshop, he was glad the door pulled in rather than needing to be pushed out. Debris piled in front of the door. The entire workshop was a mess. As they suspected, a part of the roof was torn off and was now lying against the steel beams above, bent at an odd angle. On the other side of the building, a wood plank pierced the metal siding, leaving a gaping hole around it.

Broken pottery littered the place, yet at the same time whole shelves were left standing tall with some of Emma's work still sitting on them as if they were waiting for the next step in the process. He wasn't sure how much of what was broken was done by the storm and how much was done by Marcy.

Water was pooled in spots on the floor, and rain still fell steadily inside from the hole in the roof. Other than the few areas of damaged building, the structure held up remarkably well. Noah was thankful it held.

The door to the workshop was suddenly pulled open, his brother coming through in a hurry. "Noah! Emma!" he yelled.

"We're back here, Luke," he called out in return before turning to check on Emma.

She was still passed out, either due to the head injury, the adrenaline drop, pure exhaustion or a combination of them all. Without any equipment to monitor her and the baby, he couldn't be sure. Her pulse was strong, so that was something good in her favor.

Luke appeared in the bathroom doorway as Noah bent to lift Emma up into his arms. "Is she all right? What do you need?" he asked.

"I need to get her to the hospital. She and the baby need to be checked out. I found her under a pile of crates and a shelving unit. Something hit her on the head. The bleeding has stopped, but this is the second time she's passed out," he told his brother.

"Your cars are toast. Best not to drive them. I'll bring you in and have someone stop by to secure the workshop," Luke said.

"Luke, Marcy was here in the shop when Emma showed up. She's the reason all that stuff fell on her. She attacked Emma. And Luke...she didn't make it. She was already gone by the time I found and checked on her," he said. Noah wasn't happy with the woman, but the last thing he wished for was her death.

"I'll get someone out here to take care of Marcy, but for now come with me and I'll drive you both to the hospital."

They picked their way through the debris to the door, walking through it to the drizzle outside. Looking around, Noah was amazed they had made it through the storm without more damage. Luke was right; their cars were wrecked. There was no driving them. A big tree had fallen over, smashing the roofs of both vehicles—he noted the top of the tree fell just short of the workshop. The area didn't look like anything he remembered seeing before. Pieces of metal from nearby buildings in the industrial park were strewn all over, and very few of the trees were left standing.

"I have medical kits in the trunk of my car. The keys should still be in the ignition—if they can be reached," he told his brother.

"I'll let the deputy I send out this way know. We could use them. Noah...the town didn't fare very well. The bridge is out, too. It'll be slow-going to get to the hospital," Luke said as they got into his sheriff's vehicle.

Noah couldn't bear to let Emma go, so he held her carefully on his lap in the backseat, cradling her to him. "How did you know where we were?" he asked once they were on their way.

"Sean. He called me right after he called you, but I couldn't make it over to the workshop until after the worst of the storm passed by. We were all staying put at the sheriff's office."

That made sense. He was glad his brother hadn't tried to drive to the workshop in the middle of the hurricane. From the sound of it, the town suffered a lot of damage he hadn't seen yet.

Noah was scared out of his mind. Emma still hadn't woken up. Her breathing and pulse were good, but he thought she would have woken up by now. And he didn't know how hard she fell or if any of the crates fell on her stomach.

He wouldn't know how the baby was doing until they reached the hospital and hooked her up to a monitor. Noah could have lost her and the baby. He thought he still might lose them. She may be more injured than she mentioned. He only hoped it wasn't too late to save them both.

But as much as he loved his baby already, it was nothing on how he felt about Emma. He would grieve the loss of their child, but would not be able to live without Emma. He loved her too much to ever give her up without a fight.

The lights on Luke's sheriff's vehicle flashed, and he drove as fast as possible through streets littered with debris. Noah didn't pay much attention to any of it. His attention was solely on Emma.

The brief glimpses of the town showed him there would be plenty of work to do, but none of it mattered. He only wanted to get to the hospital and hook Emma up to every machine he could think of to monitor her and the baby's health. It was most likely too much, but he had to make sure they were both healthy.

With the hospital just north of the town, the debris started to decrease as they drove. Noah couldn't believe the damage he had seen on the outskirts of town, and he wasn't so sure he wanted to see what the town proper looked like right now. But that would have to wait. Nothing was as important as Emma.

Luke pulled up at the hospital a little while later, and Noah got out with Emma. Luke had called it in beforehand, so someone was waiting on them to whisk Emma away. Noah wasn't about to let her go without him and followed them into the room. Just let them try to tell him to leave. Knowing Noah was a doctor, the others in the room didn't ask him to go, but made sure he stayed out of the way.

Noah felt like he was out of his own body. He stared at Emma the entire time willing her to wake up. Luke apparently told them she was pregnant because they had the equipment available to check on the baby. He heard the beating of his child's heart and let out a breath of relief.

Noah didn't realize how scared he was about losing the baby until he heard its heartbeat. Emma groaned and he looked at her face as her eyes fluttered open. Not wanting her to be scared when she woke up with a bunch of strangers hovering over her, he quickly walked over—moving others aside to make it through.

"It's going to be all right, Emma. You're at the hospital. Tell the doctor and nurses here what hurts," he told her, holding the hand on the arm that didn't have an IV in it.

"The baby. I had cramping while we were in the workshop," she asked in a panic.

"The baby is fine, hear the heartbeat? That's our baby," he said.

Emma relaxed immediately at his words. "I hurt all over, but mostly my shoulder and hip where the shelf hit me, and my lower legs where the shelf was lying on me when I was trapped underneath."

"Ms. Cooper, it looks like you came through with only some bumps and scrapes, but you'll most likely experience some deep bruising, too. We're going to move you to a room for observation because of that bump and cut on your head. I don't like that you passed out several times. You have a minor concussion. We'll also continue to monitor the baby. Your OB-GYN will stop in to do a more thorough checkup. Otherwise, I don't see anything concerning that a few days of rest won't help. Besides Dr. Kerrigan will probably be hovering over you for the rest of your pregnancy," the ER doctor on call said, not being able to help a little teasing in Noah's direction.

"You better believe it," Noah muttered.

49

Several days later, Emma was finally released from the hospital. She was grateful to all the visitors and to the staff and doctors, who made her stay more tolerable. Even with all the work that had to be done in Cypress Bay after Hurricane Imma came through, both of their families showed up at the hospital to check on her and the baby.

And to take care of Noah, who refused to leave her hospital room.

Everyone tried to make him leave for some food and rest, but he refused saying he would leave when she left. He had some of the nurses bring him a tray when her food was delivered and slept on a cot next to her bed. He took a quick shower in the bathroom attached to her private room, but that was the only concession he made to leaving her alone.

Now they were driving back to Cypress Bay. She was happy to be out of the hospital and that Luke and his cousin, Oliver, brought over a car for them to drive until they were able to buy new vehicles. She was still sore and bruised. Her head hurt, but it was manageable with a safe over-the-counter pain reliever she was allowed to take while pregnant. Despite all of her bumps and bruises, she was the most relieved to know their baby was doing so well.

As Noah continued driving them toward Cypress Bay, Emma saw more and more of the damage done from the storm. They all told her how bad it was while she was in the hospital, but it didn't really register until this moment. Actually seeing it for herself was unnerving. And to think it was even worse a few days ago. Since the storm blew through, everyone had already started the cleanup, but the town still looked devastated. They weren't even in the downtown area, where everyone told her the damage was worse.

"I didn't really understand how much damage there was. And now...it breaks my heart to see it this way," she murmured to Noah. Trees were down everywhere. Almost every home and business had blue tarps covering the roofs. Gas station awnings were tipped over, bent in and creased in piles of rubble.

"I know what you mean. I saw it right after the storm when we drove to the hospital, but I didn't get a good look," he replied.

While still at the hospital, Luke had come by once she was in a private room to tell them her workshop was being secured and the clinic came through the storm with no problems other than some shingle damage—most likely because it was shielded from the wind by larger buildings surrounding it.

He also told them there was roof damage at both Noah's apartment building and Emma's house. When she inquired about her brother, he assured her that Sean was good and taking care of their home.

He didn't say anything about Marcy, but she didn't expect he'd say anything when Emma was recovering from injuries caused by the woman. She didn't want to know. Noah already told her Marcy didn't make it. Emma was sad she died, but relieved she didn't need to deal with her anymore.

"Where do you want to go?" Noah asked.

"I want to go home," she responded. Noah frowned at her words before clearing his face. "And when we get there, I'd like you to help me pack up some things and take me wherever you're going to be."

Noah glanced over at Emma in surprise. Smiling at him, she placed her hand on his thigh when he turned back to watch the road. She saw him swallow hard.

"Are you sure?" he asked.

"I love you, Noah. I'm so sorry for telling you to keep us and the baby a secret. It was wrong. I should have let you shout it out to everyone. I should have told Sean myself. Not let someone else tell him. I made so many mistakes. But now I want to make us a true family, if that's what you still want," she said, holding her breath as she waited for his response. Please don't let him tell her that he changed his mind.

Pulling the car over to the side of the road, Noah gathered Emma in a hug. "I want us to be a family more than anything." He cupped her face, giving her a quick kiss on her lips, looking into her eyes filled with love.

She was surprised when he pulled one of his hands away from her face to reach around her to the glove compartment. He pulled out a small velvet box. Her eyes widened even more when she realized what he had in his hand. Noah leaned away from her a bit and opened the box while looking into her eyes.

"I had Luke pick this up from my apartment and bring it to the hospital," he said with a shrug, his mouth tipping on one side. "I love you more than anything in this world. I'd give up everything for you as long as you were in my life. Emma, would you do me the honor of marrying me? Make us the family I always dreamed about."

With tears streaming down her cheeks, she engulfed him in her arms before answering, "Yes! I love you so much."

"How long do we need to wait to get married?"

Emma laughed and pulled back at his exuberance. "Are you in a hurry?"

"I want to make you mine officially. I almost lost you, and I don't want to feel that way ever again," he said, his own tears in his eyes.

"I'm ready whenever you are," Emma replied. She expected their families would be okay with a quick wedding. She wasn't one who dreamed of big poofy dresses, lots of flowers and food. And she didn't want to wait another moment. The sooner she was Emma Kerrigan, the better.

"Come on then. Let's pack your stuff and tell Sean you're moving in with me. We'll see when the justice of the peace is available to marry us," he said as she laughed happily. He sat back in his seat and put the car in drive, merging back onto the road toward home.

50

One Month Later

Standing in her old room in her parents' home, Emma looked at herself in the mirror in what was now her mother's office. She was dressed in her wedding gown. Well, it was more of a really nice white lace dress that also accommodated her now more-than-slightly bulging stomach. She and Noah had wanted to marry right away, but realistically they knew they would need to wait.

The town had a lot of cleaning up and rebuilding to do in the aftermath of Hurricane Imma. Her parents' home had sustained some roof and garden damage, and it was the one place where she wanted to get married. The roof still had a blue tarp over it, and the gardens were a little bedraggled after the storm a month ago, but they were just as beautiful as ever after her mother spent some time cleaning them up with Emma's help.

Emma stroked her hand over her stomach. "I'm marrying your father today. We'll finally be a family, and we can't wait to meet you."

"Come in," she said at the knock on the door.

Her mother came through the doorway, followed by the Kerrigan triplets—Marinda, Katia, and Ryleigh—Demi-Lyn Shaw, Hailee Kerrigan, and Aylin Kerrigan. Aylin was the first of them all to get married and was now pregnant, finding out shortly before Emma found out about her own pregnancy. She hadn't really known the woman well, but they had started to bond over the last month—being the only two pregnant women in the bunch. She was glad she wasn't the only one and had someone she could talk to who understood all the pregnancy troubles and joys.

"You look beautiful, Emma," her mother said with tears in her eyes.

"Suck it up, Mom. Because if you cry it's all over for me and I'll cry, too," her throat already rough with emotion.

"I'm a little put out that you got into your dress already without me," Ryleigh complained teasingly, making everyone laugh.

"And that you didn't have an engagement party so we could do our color thing," Marinda said.

"Yeah, what's up with that? Noah was too sneaky and bought the ring without us knowing about it. Of course, two someone's—not mentioning any names—hid their relationship from everyone," Katia added, playfully narrowing her eyes at Emma.

"Okay, sorry for ruining all your amazing plans to mess with the guys. You did a great job with Simon and Oliver, but I'm not sad to say I'm glad it didn't work out that way for us."

"Well, we'll just need to wait for the baby shower instead then," Ryleigh said, looking over at her sisters, who gave her a nod.

Emma didn't want to think about what that was all about. They always had freaky triplet powers. Noah and Luke were similar in that they could have a complete conversation just looking at each other without actually talking. But the triplets took the prize for all the other things they seemed to just know.

"And on that note, I need to use the bathroom. Again," Aylin announced.

"I just hope I can make it through my own wedding without needing to stop into the bathroom a million times," Emma sympathized with her.

Emma's father knocked once and came into the room. "It's time to start. I'm kicking everyone out except for Emma."

Hailee handed Emma a bouquet created from the garden outside. Demi did a quick touch-up of her makeup. And the others gave her a hug before slipping out the door to find their places in the garden. Instead of chairs, they'd just have everyone stand around them as they got married.

"Look at my Emma-bean. All grown up, getting married, and having a baby," he quietly said through unshed tears.

"No crying, Dad. You're worse than Mom," she muttered. What was it with all this crying? If they didn't get moving, she'd be a huge mess before the ceremony started. "Come on, Dad, let's get me married. We can all have a cry later. After the pictures."

"Let's schedule it for the father-daughter dance then," he said. They weren't having a traditional reception that was planned to the hilt, but a dance with her father was something she wanted to do.

Her father led Emma outside to their backyard garden, where she saw Noah standing next to a trellis waiting for her. His father, Lou, who would be officiating, stood next to him. Noah was dressed in a navy blue suit with a crisp white shirt, the top button undone, and she'd thought Noah in a suit was the best sight ever.

They walked up to him, her father giving her a kiss on the cheek before leaving her with Noah and walking over to his wife.

"It's about time," Noah said with amusement, his lips quirked at the corner.

"Yeah, well, I had to talk Mom and Dad down from crying," Emma whispered with a smile of her own.

"Are you two ready?" Noah's father asked. At their nod, Luke "Lou" Kerrigan, Sr., began.

Two Months Later

Noah and a more visibly pregnant Emma were standing in front of the clinic with Dr. Mancera and his wife. Today was finally the grand reopening of the clinic. When he and Sid walked through the clinic after the storm, they found more damage than they initially thought. Water had infiltrated through some loose roof shingles, running into the walls. So they had to close down most of the clinic, other than a couple of rooms, while the damage was repaired.

Not only was Noah now the owner of the clinic—along with Dr. Mancera, his parents, and the bank until he paid them all off—it was also totally remodeled with Noah's input. He left the front waiting room area largely the same other than a fresh coat of paint.

The rest was expanded into the back lot, to include more client rooms and office space—one for a third doctor and the other for Allison, their new office manager after her promotion from intake specialist.

He also had a brand new supplies area that was only able to be accessed by him or Allison. It wasn't that he didn't trust his current doctors or nurses, but the experience with Marcy left him with a lot of sour feelings.

As the new office manager, Allison would be in charge of the whole office logistics, including ensuring all the rooms were fully stocked at all times and keeping an inventory of the supply room. With all that responsibility, she also got a nice salary increase. Noah would be depending on her to carry the clinic's operations when he couldn't be there.

In addition to the change in Allison's position, Noah hired two new doctors, a couple more nurses, and a new intake specialist for the front desk. Over the next couple of months, he'd be hiring a biller, who would handle all the insurance claims and other financial aspects of the clinic. For now, he and Allison were splitting that work themselves.

With all the extra work and a new baby on the way, he decided to cut back on his work at the hospital. It would mean getting the credentials he was working on much later than planned, but his family came first, the clinic second.

His loft apartment had sustained some damage, but his family cleaned it all up, putting a tarp on the roof before he and Emma left the hospital after the storm. Emma had moved into his apartment the day she was released, and they had been living together ever since, but it would not be ideal for long after their son was born. So they were now looking—with some help from his parents, who practically owned half of every building in Cypress Bay—for a house.

Emma's workshop wasn't as bad as they thought. Yes, she lost a lot of stock because of Marcy, but the building itself was easily repaired, and she was able to recover enough of her stock to be able to continue working without too much of a financial hit.

Of course, now that she was more advanced in her pregnancy, she spent less time in her workshop. She spent the last couple of months cleaning up, putting her workshop back together—with the help of others to rearrange and move the heavier shelving units that had fallen—and creating new stock for the shop in town. All so she could take some time off toward the end of her pregnancy and take a maternity leave after their son was born.

And that was another thing. They were having a son! Noah didn't care whether they were having a boy or a girl. But now that they found out they were having a son, he couldn't help his excitement. He cleared out the extra room in the loft apartment. Marinda, Katia, Ryleigh, Hailee, and Emma all worked their magic and turned the space into a nursery, his son's name stenciled on the wall over the crib.

Cooper Paul Kerrigan

They decided to continue the Cooper name, thinking it could be forever—if ever—that Emma's brother, Sean, had children. The name Paul was in memory of the uncle he never met, who died when he was only thirteen years old from cancer, and his paternal grandmother, Marinda Paul, who had passed away during the pandemic along with his grandfather.

"Now that you're taking over the clinic, Maggie is looking forward to traveling around a bit," Sid said to Noah about his wife, Margaret "Maggie" Mancera.

"I'll need to hire a new nurse and doctor since you're leaving me in the lurch patient load wise," he joked with the older doctor. He wasn't really joking, but he understood why Sid wanted to spend some time with his wife traveling around. He looked over at his own wife, Emma, and felt a happiness he had never really felt before.

Allison walked over to them carrying a large pair of scissors. "It's time to get started."

Noah and Sid stood in front of a large red ribbon and bow hanging in front of the clinic. Next to each of them were their wives. Allison handed the giant scissors over to the men, then walked over to a podium, waiting for them to give the signal.

Looking out over the crowd, Noah saw everyone he cared about was in attendance—his parents, brother, cousins and their families, aunts, uncles; Emma's parents and brother; friends and community members. And he felt like his life couldn't get any better.

Then he looked over at Emma once again, reminding himself that life would be getting better soon when his son was born.

Giving a nod to his office manager, she announced the grand re-opening of the clinic under the new ownership of Dr. Noah Kerrigan.

EPILOGUE

Sheriff Luke Kerrigan, Jr., stood in front of the clinic watching his twin brother start a new chapter in his life. A new wife, a soon-to-be-born son, taking over ownership of the clinic. A sense of unease washed over him as though he was missing out on something in his own life. He couldn't have what Noah had. They may be identical twins, but their lives had gone in directions so opposite from each other. His brother was built for the family life. Luke was not. His past experiences made sure of that.

As the grand reopening ceremony wound down, everyone started to disburse from in front of the clinic. Town citizens walked to their cars or to the other shops in the downtown area.

He reflected on how his extended family was going about their own lives—some starting their own families now and others still as single as he was. It was humbling to notice that all the male cousins except for him, were now married or engaged. The only other cousins that were single were the triplets and Hailee.

How did he become the last remaining single male cousin?

He thought they'd all be single together for a long time to come. Who knew that Simon, Oliver, and Noah would now be part of a couple, with two of them about to have their own kids. He never saw it coming. Oh, he knew it would happen eventually, but never thought it would happen so soon or that they would start falling one after the other like they did.

Luke prepared to say his goodbyes to his brother and sister-in-law before going back to work. As he was about to leave, a car came speeding up to the curb, parking haphazardly. He was spitting mad! The person could have killed someone driving like that! If it had been even a few minutes earlier, the entire parking lot in front of the clinic would have been filled with people.

Whoever was driving this car should be locked up for driving so recklessly. And he was going to go tell them so right this moment.

As he prepared to rush over to yell at the driver—and give the reckless driver a ticket—he saw the woman who just moved into Demi-Lyn's place rush out of the driver's seat. She ran to the back, grabbing a small boy out of the backseat.

Luke quickly sized up the situation and realized the boy was crying, holding his arm, while his mother was in panic mode. His temper was immediately squashed at what he now understood was a frantic mother trying to get help for her injured son.

Calling over his shoulder to Noah, he rushed forward to Gracie—yes; he knew her name. How could he not. He stood in her way, putting his hand on her shoulders to stop her from running and tripping over the curb.

Her panicked look had him reassuring her. "Gracie, everything will be all right. Take a deep breath and calm down so we can go inside and help your son." He saw her panic was also affecting her son. He was crying harder now, though it might also be due to the pain of being moved.

His words had the effect he was hoping for. She looked up at him and took a deep breath, then nodded. Luke wanted to take the boy out of Gracie's arms, but knew he would have to pry him out with the mama bear look she had going on right then. Sure, she was panicking, but she also had a look that said if anyone touched her boy, he was a dead man. Luke directed Gracie into the clinic and a patient room, where Noah was waiting for them.

"What happened?" Noah asked as Luke encouraged her to put the boy down on the table.

"Sebastian was playing outside when I heard him scream. I think he broke his arm trying to climb a tree," she told Noah.

As Noah examined the boy, he kept giving Luke a confused look. He knew Noah was wondering why he was still at the clinic. He couldn't really explain it either. There was something about Gracie that made him want to make sure she was safe. And for some reason, that extended to her son, too. Not understanding why he felt that way, he vowed to stick close until he figured it out. Even if it meant insinuating himself into Gracie's life.

Thank you for reading **Always Been You**! Your recommendations and reviews would be greatly appreciated—they mean so much to indie authors.

Want more? Find out what happens between Luke and Gracie in It Had To Be You:

Sheriff Luke Kerrigan was juggling the chaos left in the wake of a hurricane and the shady crew hired to rebuild Cypress Bay's bridge. The last thing he expected was to be drawn to the guarded woman staying in town with her young son.

Gracie Acton-Rogers just wanted to keep Sebastian safe from the wealthy in-laws who saw him as their heir. But when one reckless night leads to her son's kidnapping, Luke risks everything to bring him home—and to prove some risks are worth taking.

Available April 2026: https://andreafinnelly.com/book/it-had-to-be-you/

Curious about how the Kerrigans got started in Cypress Bay? Get an exclusive prequel, Founding Hearts, about John and Marinda Kerrigan, the grandparents of The Kerrigan Family by signing up for my newsletter at www.andreafinnelly.com.

ABOUT THE AUTHOR

Andrea Finnelly writes both contemporary romantic suspense and paranormal fantasy romance—two genres that let her explore everything from small-town danger to otherworldly magic. Her debut series, The Kerrigan Family, follows eight siblings and cousins as they navigate love and the hazards that pursue them.

Originally from New England, she now lives in the South, where hurricanes and heat waves are wearing out their welcome. When Andrea's not writing, she's watching hockey, auto racing, Doctor Who, home improvement, and paranormal shows. She also loves curling up on her couch to read, and scanning homes for sale in a climate that's cooler and without a lot of snow.

For more books and updates:
www.andreafinnelly.com

ALSO BY ANDREA FINNELLY

The Kerrigan Family Series

Founding Hearts: John & Marinda (Exclusive subscriber prequel)

Better With You: Simon & Aylin

Coming Home To You: Oliver & Demi-Lyn

Always Been You: Noah & Emma (January 2026)

It Had To Be You: Luke & Gracie (April 2026)

Hooked On You: Hailee & Joel (July 2026)

Finding Home With You: Marinda & Sean (October 2026)

Falling For You: Ryleigh & Dillon (January 2027)

Then There Was You: Katia & Beck (April 2027)